Day Job

· · · · ·

Day Job

· · · · ·

A Workplace Reader
for the
Restless Age

Jonathan Baird

with additional readings selected by Carol M. Allen

ALLEN
— & —
OSBORNE
Inc.

An Allen & Osborne Book

———

Created and Produced by
Allen & Osborne, Inc.
148 State Street
Boston, MA 02109

10 9 8 7 6 5 4 3 2

Library of Congress Catalog Card Number: 97-80473
Baird, Jonathan
Day Job: A Workplace Reader for the Restless Age

Includes bibliographical references and notes.
ISBN 0-9660805-2-1
1. Business. 2. Pop Culture.

Cover design by Jonathan Baird.
Cover photograph furnished by Tony Stone Images, Inc.

Printed in China

LON!

- CS Manager and scourge; preserved by the stresses of his middle-mgmt post in a state of unease so acute you might call it embattlement; the whining of tiny and greatly overtaxed machinery a near-audible undercurrent to speech

- Full load of black body hair revealed at summer outing; gauntlets of it for forearms and the backs of hands, great fans across chest, leggings down to mid-calf, a stout-looking collar for back of his neck; like some garment the American Colonists might have found fashionable

This way to Meeting Concourse, Production Floor   FOOT TRAFFIC

MARK RATTNER

- Not the Mark Rattner from "Fast Times," but name is the first of many parallels, second being his looks
- 5 yrs. on the job; breakdown judged to be forthcoming; Rattner is monitored like San Andreas and prodded by thrillseekers
- Broad repertoire of overdone impersonations: golden-age celebs (Bogart, Cagney, Jimmy Stewart); presidents (Nixon, Reagan); etc.

DOROTHY SPAINER

- American-born but returned from English adolescence with accent; maintains it in order to affect intelligence
- Self-styled patrician doing time here as others might have tried the Peace Corps, awaited by grand and richly-deserved destiny; nobody else buying this, of course
- At summer outing, refused to order beers at bar, only "poynts"

14 in. gap, must be negotiated sideways

STRUCTURAL
SUPPORT
COLUMN

<----->

MARIA ALVAREZ

- Cube decked with latino Christmas decorations the year round
- Husband is bodybuilding bakery hand, homicidally jealous; if Maria's aware of any other conversation topic she doesn't let on
- Bored, uppity 9-yr.-old son left here MWF at 5:30; nearly electrocuted (accident?) building a 'fort' near file-server station

ME

- Leading tricky double-life of day worker/bon vivant
- Post-college honeymoon irrecoverably past; now either traversing pre-career threshold or wandering trackless abyss
- Unable to completely embrace or reject the necessity of work
- Waiting here for something better

FOOT TRAFFIC

EMPTY WORK STATION

- Equipment left idle 90% of the time while we look on from vastly inferior machines

SURLY DESIGN FREELANCER STATIONED HERE THIS A.M.

- Fears quality of work will flag from prolonged exposure to 'non-creative atmosphere'

TRACI VENDLER, HR PRINCESS

- Arrested, knowingly and gleefully; in "breathless 17-year-old" developmental stage
- Capable of pathology-grade optimism and verve, conversations of astonishing volume and duration
- Attended everywhere by faintest smell of wet dog; those around her are aware of nothing immediate but can't escape the impression that somewhere, far off perhaps, there are wet dogs at play

CLAY PIRNER'S OFFICE (SALES)

This way to Offices of Senior Management ➤

FOOT TRAFFIC ➤

This way to Sales, Accounting, Reception ➤

DIERDRE PENMARTIN

- 'Miss Hospital-Corners'; aggressive, formidable perkiness and poise; helmet-like Junior League bob gives weird impression of removability
- Led charge against D. Ritchie after his loutish display at co. outing
- Addresses all men as 7-year-old boys; is not only accepting of, but charmed by, our perceived incompetence and vulgarity

JASON PITCHER

- Tireless pessimist and font of sarcasm; gothic malcontent
- Ally and confidant of the unwary and malleable
- Champion of honesty, reason, candor, other ill-advised values/behaviors; either following doctrines of conscience here or just trying to make trouble

KEVIN SWINDELL

- Tall, pinkish, fair, sharp dresser; airtight veneer of good humor breeds dept.-wide mistrust of him
- Private life either corrupt and outlandish or insufferably dull
- Wife Kay did all the outgoing recordings for our co. voicemail system; late-nite DJ-type voice—Kay is one woman I'd marry sight-unseen

KENDRA SHANNAHAN

- Mountainous juggernaut of a woman; dangerous combo of size and reckless animation; less an accident waiting to happen than one perpetually in progress
- Practical joke enthusiast: squirt nickels, rubber mice, vanishing ink
- Defiantly snaggletoothed in an age of orthodontics

CHARLENE TUNNEY

- Rangy, taciturn, pale, haunted waif; appears to have survived own embalming; we exchange 2 or 3 words a week, on avg.
- Reason for her hire to CS as unfathomable as her decision to apply in the first place
- Brother-in-law Dennis hung self from a swing set

DESMOND RITCHIE

- 3 mo.'s on CS team; 'bumbling newcomer' aura sustained by abject lack of common sense
- Thought cloud above head contains unmodified version of whatever he happens to be looking at
- Immoderate drinking at summer outing draws censure co.-wide; has also gained him cult figure status among office reprobates

FOOT TRAFFIC ➤

AMBIGUOUS "UTILITY" AREA, BOILER ROOM OR AC UNIT, WHO KNOWS

- Source of continual throbbing white noise; sound has eerily organic quality
- Sounds of mechanical stress augur industrial accident
- Racket has made a slum of neighboring cubes, where newcomers are typically stationed

I

. . . .

9:34 AM

Well sit right down my evil son and let me tell you a story.

—— Black Francis

. . . .

*F*irst come the outgoing stragglers from third shift, eyes leveled
at the revolving door I've left in motion. We pass in the lobby,
nine floors down from our office, fey and wall-eyed as one another.
When they ask me what it's like outside, they don't mean the weather,
they mean what are things like outside of this building. As though
the world has been taken apart and reconstituted while they were on
shift, and they can be certain of nothing remaining from days previous. I feed them fantastic information like 'someone has taken all
the cars.' Which is news they seem to have expected: they nod along,
grim and resigned. Actually they're paying no more attention to me
than to those men selling magazines and caramelized nuts. At 9:30 in
the morning, the third shift mind recognizes words like door and
train and bed, and simple active verbs like go; otherwise they just
nod in the direction of speech.

The elevator, like the subway, is pretty well depopulated.
Securing the top button of my work shirt now, and starting to thread
a tie through the collar. I press floor 9 exactly once. There are
four of us in here, mostly clearing throats and consulting watches. Footfalls accelerate across the lobby
and we study the door-open button until we're closed
in--except we're not, there's a French cuff lodged
between the doors, a man's fist in it making an
aggressive display of his college class ring. We
fall back as far as the little recess allows.

Here comes a badly winded, pomaded hardballer in a
herringbone suit, who steps in and executes a military-style pivot,
bends at the waist and starts hammering on the floor 3 button like
to beat all hell. Suddenly no room to deal with my tie, and I've got
to let it trail down my shirtfront. Our man's still hitting that
button when we land on 3, where he regains his height, shoots his
cuffs, and thumbs his sunglasses back onto the bridge of his nose.
Then it's off past his receptionist and no 'Good morning' for her
either, he just says "Damn" at his watch. "Oh-kay" someone ventures
when he's gone, and throats are cleared again.

Space, finally, to wind my tie around into a knot, but I'm down
to about 90 seconds. No surprises when it comes out like some
deranged cousin of the four-in-hand.

8

The young man is kicked through all the centuries: boys who know nothing of war, diplomacy, or commerce are considered fit to be introduced to political history. We moderns also run through art galleries and hear concerts in the same way as the young man runs through history. We can feel that one thing sounds differently from another, and pronounce on the different "effects." And the power of gradually losing all feelings of strangeness or astonishment, and finally being pleased at anything, is called the historical sense, or historical culture. The crowd of influences streaming on the young soul is so great, the clods of barbarism and violence flung at him so strange and overwhelming, that an assumed stupidity is his only refuge. Where there is a subtler and stronger self-consciousness we find another emotion too—disgust. The young man has become homeless: he doubts all ideas, all moralities.

| REF. NO. | *See notes, pp. 148-151* | AUTHOR(S) | **Friedrich Nietzsche** |

...if you can abide the universal masculine...

Ahem. Our cheery 'new' reception area. The one we occupied in March, that in July's still lousy with flowers and congratulatory mailings from our clients, unsunk nailheads and unsanded gouts of spackle, the sawdust smells of new construction.

"...though some of us just drop in when we feel like it, isn't that right, Mark?" sez Holly.

"Blah blah blah" is my Bond-Moneypenny riposte.

"Mmm-hmm, anyways you learn it's best to ignore the junior staff, they're mainly brats like him and if you see them out here it means they're trying to kill time." She's speaking to a temp in Carl's seat whose name also happens to be Holly, and whose looks would make you think of a ruined starlet. Our Holly's tone suggests that this is a training session. "If you don't know who's who, just look at how they're dressed. Khakis and a white shirt with no jacket, if they look like him, like an ice-cream man, pay no attention, okay? Don't even look up unless you want to."

"Wha? I—" too tired for this.

The temp swivels, slow and automatic, in her chair to regard me without any expression at all. "He missed a beltloop," she says. "Heh-heh." Out pokes her lower lip. "What's that you're writing?"

I'm actually writing *What's that you're writing?*, but there's no point in telling her so. Too early to be fielding questions on the Journal, thank you.

"This? We're supposed to jot something down if we feel Holly here's getting too uppity. Part of her therapy. She should probably explain it herself," which is Holly's, the first one's, cue to start jabbering in real earnest. The temp stays planted next to her, trained on my notebook, still with the sprung bottom lip. Looks like she's been left in that chair unplugged.

There's a man in coveralls behind me, too. He's busy tapping the floor for joists, drilling, blowing the filings from his bit, tapping and drilling some more. This is the routine he's been at since Monday, indicating, I think, that he's a prop. They probably keep him out here like the flowers and the spackle lest anyone forget about our build-out. After all, it's been over a month since

9

Excerpted by William James over a hundred years ago. Seems not to have gone out of date.

"From work like ours there seems to us to have been eliminated every element which constitutes the nobility of labor. We feel no personal pride in its progress, and no community of interest with our employer. There is none of the joy of responsibility, none of the sense of achievement, only the dull monotony of grinding toil, with the longing for the signal to quit work, and for our wages at the end.

"And being what we are, the dregs of the labor-market, and having no certainty of permanent employment, and no organization among ourselves, we must expect to work under the watchful eye of a gang-boss, and be driven, like the wage-slaves that we are, through our tasks."

REF. NO. 2 *See notes, pp. 148-151* **AUTHOR(S)** **Walter Wyckoff**

those <u>Here We "Grow" Again!!</u> mailers went out, and our clients might need some reminding that we're the company on the move, that we're still growing to serve them better, reaching out into the millennium and all that.

I try dishing with Holly and the other Holly--already forgotten what about--until whatever I've said about somebody (Annette Funicello?) earns me an evil eye from both of them, and the salaried Holly tells me I ought to get to work.

Okay. Heading in through reception, is my point here, rather than the less-conspicuous shipping desk. The word this morning is 'unabashed.' Well and 'late' too, obviously. As in, I'm <u>late</u> to work and effect an entrance that is <u>unabashed</u>. Greeting people full-on in the hallway off reception. Good morning, a-yep, just got here, thanks. This is the hall they'd originally lined with bright burgundy wallpaper, flocked paper actually, with a pattern like you'd expect to find in a Chinese restaurant or a bordello. Impossible now to find out whose idea that was. And a swirl ceiling too. It was brilliant, which is a way of saying it was hugely controversial and short-lived. The paint overhead hadn't even dried when they put in the standard drop-ceiling. They stripped the wallpaper soon afterward and replaced it with a rick-rack wall, where they've hung a gauntlet of motivational placards. These are succeeding each other now on my right like the old Burma-Shave billboards:

<u>Fig. I.1</u>

<u>Rick-rack wall off of reception</u>

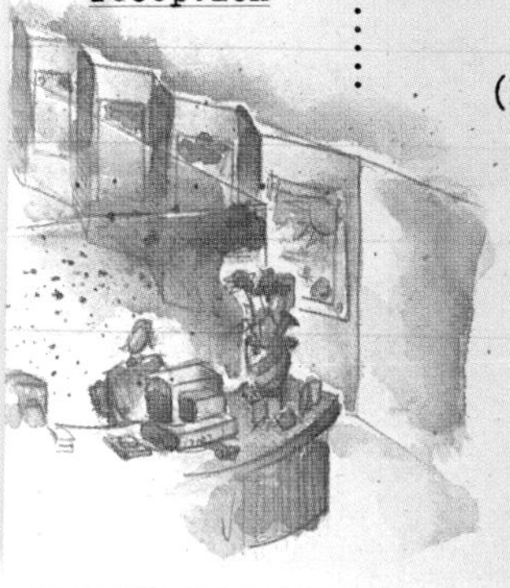

"How Do You Feel?" the first one would like to know. (Like I've been dragged in here behind a truck). "Alive, Energetic, Interested..." the second has decided. The third's a little more assertive: "Motivated! Dedicated! Creative!" And the last, poetically: "How Do You Feel?" They're supposed to change these diabolic little signs every month, but they've seen fit to preserve 'How Do You Feel' since midwinter. As top-down motivational messaging goes, it must be hard to improve on.

So this is your fun-house conveyance to the back office. The little hall opens out to a vista of corporate gunmetal grey, the cubicles and offices of company headquarters. And none of your New Age *Feng Shui* here! No indeed. They've hemmed bodies into workstations with the kind of fore-thought you'd use in filling an icetray. Visitors from another time or civilization wouldn't believe, I don't think, that we'd not only built this place for ourselves, but intended to stay. Like the Anasazi in their cliff dwellings. But we've been nowhere else for 7 years now, billeted in between these fabric-jacketed pressboard walls and painted-metal stanchions, can-tilevered bookshelves and formica work surfaces, perched on our grey low-back swivel chairs and wheeling across these studded plastic mats. Everything as regular and right-angled as an architectural plan risen to life (or nearly to life)—wall, cube, floor, ceiling, and, occasionally, window. The air too takes on that rarified, hospital-ward quality. And the punchline is, these company captains out patrolling the halls and ushering their staffs into place are certain that the Golgotha they've made here is the home of productivity and concert, that only in a setting this bleak will the employee find refuge from lassitude and distraction....

People are using the PA about as judiciously as ever—Martha your 9:45 is here early, can anyone tell Steve Schimmer where his client on 106 has gone, Gary is stepping out for 10 or 15 minutes okay, there's a courier in shipping, umm, who's it for? Blah, blah, blah. Phones are going off in lit-tle electronic volleys, some keyboards and mice are getting bullied around, that's about it for noise.

A quarter mile or so from here, this corridor flares out into the amphitheater-style conference area where we mass for TQM meetings and other large-scale enactments of corporate ritual. Plenty of people to pass on the way of course. Hello, good morning, hello, yes yes. There isn't a Senior Staffer who won't pull an elaborate double-take to his or her wristwatch. Yeah you're damn right I'm late.

Lined up into the distance are the offices of middle management. They're in there pacing and typing, sharpening pencils, threatening peo-ple on the phone. Outside, stained lengths of pine are mitred around the grey doors and louvre-blinded windows that recur in pairs. Save for Clay Pirner's, where he's forced a paperback mystery into the hinge, all the office doors stay closed. The walls are spatter-painted grey, deep grey and black, flecked microscopically grey-blue, grey-green and rust. And festooned with all manner of company propaganda—departmental mis-sion statements and success stories and bon mots; aphorisms of industry wizards and sports heroes, expensively reproduced; hamhanded client let-ters and industry awards and (what else?) the firing-squad portraits of

Everyone's monitors face out toward foot traffic, meaning the forbidden fruits of the Internet may be sampled only at tremendous personal risk. Which is more of a concern for some than others, of course. We had a French intern not only download but print out 3 or 4 pages of celebrity nudes, and this before he'd had his network tutorial. I remember him pacing like a hen around accounting's laserwriter while his files were coming up on the production floor. Big laffs for an hour or two before Senior Management got around to firing him.

our employees of the month. Want to see someone rising to challenge, rallying against the odds, mastering setback? Here's 5'9" Spudd Webb dunking on a regulation hoop. Outside the sales office, Clay's hung a fever chart of his team targets and actuals, and recycled that header from our post-card, Here We "Grow" Again!!, with that same flourish of punctuation.

Rounding the horn toward my workstation now (see customer service plan view) when I sidestep and fetch Rattner a smart dope-slap on the back of his head. And with that institutional haircut of his, it doesn't take much wrist to get a gratifying *snap!* He lets a little hiss escape from his mouth, which means he's not feeling too playful yet; he'll be game enough in 15 minutes, when I'm on the phone and one of his oranges comes bouncing, very playfully indeed, off the crown of my head.

It's 9:44 when I face into my cube for the first time and...and I decide someone's been in here. Not because it seems to have been been ran-sacked, it's the opposite, like some of this might have been __arranged__: I may have tucked my chair in tight like that to the desk, *or* someone may have forced it in so they could stand over it and type. Same with the phone cord, seems to have been pulled taut and re-coiled just a little too per-fectly, and that's an improbable angle for my key-board, isn't it—all right, I'm positive now. And I really am considering a line about 'sensing' someone else in my cube, when I notice Lon stand-ing behind me.

Your bosses have angered the gods of Feng Shui.

Avoid having your desk directly in line with the door or sitting with your back to a window, because these factors will weaken your position. Never sit with your back to the door when you are working. Part of your awareness will always be tied up in sensing whether someone has come up behind you, and your nerves, productivity, and efficiency will all suffer as a result. If sitting in this position is unavoidable, a Feng Shui cure is to hang a mirror above the desk to reflect people approaching you from behind.

| REF. NO. 3) | *See notes, pp. 148-151* | AUTHOR(S) | Karen Kingston |

9:44 AM -- Ambushed by Lon

Billy the Kid, who was smart, used to sit facing out from corners. I spin around a little late to see Lon Baffert, who's equally surprised to find me here.

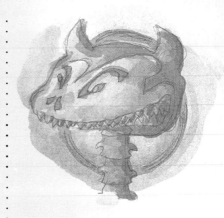

Fig. I.2
Meet the Boss! Lon Baffert

It's a typically oblique entrance for Lon, whose slightness of figure and neutrality of dress give him the annoying advantage of stealth. The idea with Lon is that you don't so much notice him as become slowly aware of him, like you'd sense some obscure and unsettling detail, a picture that's fallen askew or a bird that's stolen in and been watching you from a high vantage. Even when you're looking dead at him he's hard to fix, mostly because there's not much to him, 5'6" is all, lean and dissipated as a marathoner. What human jerky would look like if they were to make such a thing.

But you've got to ignore your instincts and take this little man seriously. Or I do, I should say, he's my boss. Lon's the guy who not only administers my professional fate, but who runs the whole customer service rodeo, 10 of us in all. And that, along with being one of the crueller conditions of my life, accounts for much of what's wrong with Lon.

"Hey-hey, glad you could join us this morning, Mark." His index finger, flagged with a bright yellow post-it, is held awkwardly aloft.

Authority in this office is feudalized into three tiers. A 10-executive star chamber called Senior Management eats highest on the hog, all interdepartmental powermongers, Vice Presidents, Senior Vice Presidents, a President and 4 owners. The middle managers, 30 to 40-year-old careerist group heads like Lon, form the thin buffer of the second tier. And then there's the junior infantry, predominantly recent college grads who cycle through here on one- and two-year tours of duty. The model works like this: the irresistible force of senior-level authority rails at the immovable object of junior-level apathy. One group forces the office toward a civilian militarism, the other toward irremediable discord. And the limbo between is the difficult terrain of middle management.

Jason Pitcher likens it to Goya's painting 'Two Men With Cudgels,' where two men are pounding each other with wood mallets as they both sink into a bog. Except in this model there are three men, two with cudgels and one without, and the two armed men are beating

13

on the third, or the middle manager, in the way they might drive a railroad spike.

The conceit holds, certainly, for customer service: when Senior Management catches the first glimmer of client dissatisfaction, they come right after Lon. And Lon, being our most immediate and accessible symbol of corporate authority, is where we focus whatever anger and derision we can safely marshal. All of which has lent him that interrogation-victim twitchiness of his, that ceaseless animation of the eyes and hands. You can see the full array of cords on his neck, the sinew laid in little ropes along his arms, the veins and tendons in his wrists and on the backs of his bird-hands, all like pages out of Gray's Anatomy. Everything strained and gnarled like the dark residue from a more robust version of himself. Point is, if he looks like he's been fed through the gears of some horrible machine, well, he has.

"My train, I mean I was running late anyway Lon, but I sat for a good 15 minutes on the platform before it rolled in. I don't know, getting serviced or whatever, one of those schedule delays..."

Lon, not stupid, is having none of this. He just sticks the post-it to my counter and waits for me to give up. Note reads: "My office when you get in.--Lon."

"Just a quickie," he sez. "When you get a minute."

"Uh, I've got one now...?"

Lon tries for a cogitative look, to mask a more obvious displeasure. He was going to leave his note here for me and get some coffee, give me some time to get worked up before I finally came to his office wringing a hat in my hands. Now he's stranded himself in the CS bullpen, the rest of the team in earshot and attending closely. If he leads me back to his office this will qualify as an 'incident,' and I doubt it's anything that serious. That spicy, licorice smell that follows him around is slowly gathering mass in my cube.

"All right, sure." Lon stares absently at my guest chair but continues to stand. "I was walking by this station 10 minutes ago, noticed it was empty, heard the phone ringing. It was what, 9:30? Now that's a perfectly reasonable time for a client to call. Ditto from 5:30 to 6. I just happened to be there to pick it up. It was Mary Heidseck looking for her film, said it was supposed to be waiting for her this morning, it wasn't, obviously, and she was looking for you."

"Let's get this straight, Lon, I don't care about Mary Heidseck. Or her film," is what I can't manage to say next. Instead, I'm avoiding his eyes, shifting in my chair, that whole bit. Only hope he's feeling as awkward as I am. Which looks to be the case--like I say, I've caught him off guard too, he hadn't known I was in yet but I was, I am, and now I'm seated at my own desk and he's the one standing with nowhere really to prop an elbow.

14

"I was able to run some interference which, that's no problem," he's saying. "You still owe her a call but...anyway, no big deal. Bottom line is, I can't have your clients stuck in voice-mail when they call in pissed. Or transferred to another rep who isn't familiar with the job. We make a practice of that, we go out of business. Right?"

"Uh-huh."

"Now let me say to you something Jay Gathers told me in facilitation training: he said if you load a regular household candle into a shotgun, you can blast it right through an oak board. Imagine? Just a cylinder of wax, with the right attitude, penetrates solid oak. Makes you think..."

"—"

"...Okay, what does that make you think? Like in light of this situation we're having right now?" Up with the eyebrows.

"Yes I know, I know. If I keep showing up late in the morning you'll have to blast me through a board."

"Wha? No, ah-Mark, that isn't the point at all. See, the point is, is that given the right motivators, you're going to see things happen to your on-the-job performance that you can't even imagine yet. Now, for now, getting you in here on time"—my phone starts ringing—"that's where we start. You're in on time, every day. 9:15 or 9:30? Nah-ah. From now on you're settled in, taking calls by then. Zero tolerance means no excuses. That begins today."

"Right, I'm sorry you even have to—"

"That's not even the Quality Commitment, understand, that's basics. Follow? Good. Now 10:45, one hour from now—what happens then?"

"Team meeting." Phone continuing, of course, to ring.

"R-r-right. Team meeting, I'm reminding everyone. So...you ready for this call, Thornton?"

"Uh-huh." One more ring and whoever it is gets bounced back to reception, though.

"You psyched?"

"Yes, uh-huh."

Lon gives me a significant look. "Alright then, let's go. Snap some crackers."

"Hello, this is Mark," I say evenly. It's a dial tone. Lon withdraws, giving me the thumbs-up.

Jay Gathers, TQM Grand Wizard, is dropping in this afternoon to rally the faithful. He's meeting at 3:30 with Senior Management and other high-ranking invertebrates, before they open it up to a general office assembly from 5:00 to who knows when. Depends how many of us act up in the Q+A.

15

The 1980s witnessed the spectacular rise of management schools, consultants, media, and gurus who fed on the insecurities of American managers fearful of foreign competition and economic decline. Mistrustful of their own judgment, many managers latched on to these self-appointed pundits, readily adopting their latest panaceas. Off-the-shelf programs addressing quality, customer satisfaction, time-to-market, strategic focus, core competencies, alliances, global competitiveness, organizational culture, and empowerment swept through U.S. corporations with alarming speed.

Adopting "new" ideas became a way for companies to signal to the world that they were progressive, that they had come to grips with their misguided pasts, and that they were committed to change.... But in the majority of cases, research shows, the management fads of the last 15 years rarely produced the promised results.... What accounts for such disastrous results? We believe it is the failure of U.S. management to address its most serious problem: a lack of pragmatic judgment.... Instead of subscribing impulsively to fads, [managers] must pick and choose carefully the managerial ideas that promise to be useful. And they must adapt those ideas rigorously to the context of their companies. Managers will often profit most by resisting new ideas entirely and making do with the materials at hand.

REF. NO. *4*) **AUTHOR(S)** **Nitin Nohria and James D. Berkley**

9:50 AM -- TQM From the Mouths of Babes

TQM = Total Quality Management. Equals self-induced delirium endemic to the workplace, cultured in Japan and bred there into management teams, by an American no less, and since exported back to the U.S. where, like kudzu, its spread has been difficult to contain. Human hosts exhibit artificially--often dangerously--elevated levels of team spirit, and may succumb to fits of mindless productivity. When assembled, groups of contaminated individuals lapse into loud and ungovernable fugue-like states, wherein future trends of commerce are prophesied and cosmic lessons in human behavior are thought to reveal themselves. Amidst their fellows in the TQM saturnalia, devotees are known not only to speak in tongues but to converse: bizarrities like proaction, deconstruct, ideate, rubric, walking the talk, infrastructure, value-added and consensus-building are exchanged as though real meanings were attached to these words....

TQM began taking root here six months before my hire, so that by the time I came to work, Senior Management had the hammer down good. One of our big blue-chip clients is a manufacturer of analog film processors, and they'd had so much success with the program, they invited our Senior Management team over to kick its tires. Sounds like our people were snakebit. They heard how TQM had fattened up the Michigan auto barons, and, after all, how much difference was there really between a service bureau staff

Actually ← TQM was developed in America! It was largely ignored here for 40 years, and only put into practice after some fairly dramatic successes in Japan.

16

like their own and those assembly-line robots in Detroit?

   Before long, it was TQM everything back home. First came a flurry of
memos proclaiming "excitement" to be "in the air," meaning we'd better
brace for a sweeping top-down decree from management. After a couple more
weeks they fixed all their nonspecific threats with the face of TQM and
began the siege in earnest: here were the productivity secrets of the
future given unto us today; one painless week of seminars would make all
of us, individually and collectively, successful beyond fantasy; doors
were going to burst wide before us and all the paths to market domination
would be laid plain. In other words, Senior Management had decided on a
new way for their employees to behave. It was their company, and if they
wanted the culture here upended in a blitzkrieg of re-training sessions,
all they had to do was post beginning and end dates.

   Middle management surprised no one when they went up like a prairie
fire. They thought this was the reinvention of the management wheel.
Managers started acting like they do now, which is like their heads have
been carved out and refilled with something that Jay Gathers can operate
by remote. They took on the Heaven's-Gate glaze we'd seen on the Seniors,
and that alien vocabulary too--snapping crackers, candles and boards, zero
tolerance, that business. Now if you stomped on one manager's foot the
rest would cry out; if you killed one, two would spring up in his place.
Rebby Conlon and a few others held on to a measure of free will but easily half, our Lon included, became instant hard-core converts. These were
our "bridge facilitators," or less formally the TQM Bastard Squad.

   As for the rest of us, down on the fat end of the personnel wedge
(where we tend to have a healthy respect and fear for these Moses-on-the-
Mount type decrees), the reception wasn't much warmer than
luke-. Anything management would seize on with this kind
of alacrity couldn't be good for us, was the idea. But
what was eerie about their counter-response was that
there wasn't one to speak of. They'd been forewarned
about objections, styled "growing pains" now,
but they were likewise convinced of TQM's
inevitability. Training sessions were sched-
uled and posted, employees slotted into them,
attendance was taken and that was that. Dissent
was welcomed into the TQM meeting, where it could
be run through the "objection cycle" and neatly outflanked.
Objections weren't threats to the model at all, they actually helped
demonstrate how it worked.

   TQM was built, said Jay Gathers, to withstand anything short of full-
scale employee rejection. Which wouldn't happen when acceptance of the
program was linked to job security. That is, you either rallied behind

TQM or your name showed up on someone's ledger. A pair of hired
goons calling themselves a "TQM tactical unit" would pay you a
visit and if they couldn't get you on board, well, Senior
Management would learn that you were standing in the way of
progress. We had a number of holdouts, and 2 or 3 not-unimportant
people left the company, but this too was considered healthy,
eggs broken to render the better omelette.

This fact that the seeds of corruption are buried in the causes of improvement strikes us everywhere in the political, moral, and natural history of the world. It seems to indicate the intentions of
Providence to limit human perfectibility and to bind together good and evil like life and death by
indissoluble connection.

REF. NO. 5) *See notes, pp. 148-151*   AUTHOR(S) **Ralph Waldo Emerson**

. . . .

The most dangerous things in the world are immense accumulations of human beings who are manip-
ulated by only a few heads.

Carl G. Jung

        Much more to the TQM story, of course, just needed a quick backdrop for
the real beginning of the story--or how I got involved in this Journal
business in the first place. How a self-improvement initiative that could-
n't have been more unlike TQM was sold in that guise to management; how
the comedy that birthed this thing would, in the space of a 15-minute
meeting, turn cruel enough to be taken for tragedy....
        A client of mine had gone through the Journal program a month or so
prior to this writing, and she'd come in proselytizing. This was a
woman who used to send us calendars with her deadline days wreathed in
a hundred exclamation points, who liked to threaten to come in and run
our machines herself, and here she was, recommending self-help titles to
me and saying imprecise things like "whenever you get around to it."
She was dressing better and, I've got to say, she seemed to be enjoying
her life a great deal more. And like any good zealot, she felt it terribly important that I follow her example, and she gave me a number to
call (she tried a handful of our managers too, but her 'awakening' was
roundly dismissed as some menopausal side-effect).
        I bought it, though, enough to contact you people--you at SysCorp,
that is, who are reading this now, and getting ready to write your notes
in the margins and all that. Got the immediate impression of a downtown

startup, though I was told you'd been at it for some 20 years now. I envisioned your staff as a bookish gang of liberal arts grads, not bohemian really but on the 'unkempt' side of straight, in there with a university-caliber library and mystics and wise men herded in from all over the place. The rep I talked to (Brian?) was uncomfortable classifying the Journal as a 'management program'—

"That's just our marketing language, that's how we're forced to sell it. CEOs and managers won't buy a package that doesn't promise results, like profit margin results, so that's what we put on the block. And it <u>does</u>, the Journal's been proven to boost performance, we've got all kinds of numbers on that. But earning your bosses more money, we think of that like a desirable side-effect rather than our main point of business. We focus on a broader picture for the individual, you know, life, career, success, 'right livelihood' is the term I hear a lot...."

He asked me to characterize both the management culture and the state of morale here. I told him about TQM and '2 Men with Cudgels.' He made me repeat 'TQM' twice more; I might as easily have told him we were fashioning arrowheads out of bits of flint over here. 'Antediluvian' was the word he used. Seems the company of tomorrow's blasting into the future with a program that died around 1994.

"So you're up and running with TQM, or are you still in transition there?"

"Depends who you ask. I think our managers would say we're all in this with both feet. And I think they really believe that."

"Because the thing is, we're called in most often when a competing management program's already in place, one imported from an outside consulting group like your Dr. Gathers', we get called in to do damage control. Digging corporations back out of those outmoded or misapplied team-based models, it's becoming a specialty of ours. The dogs called in to rid the house of the cats that were brought in for the mice, you've heard that story."

Anyhow, I was sold. I told him I'd be pitching this to my managers and could he please send along some self-promo materials for my proposal. There followed a 2 or 3 day onslaught of SysCorp pamphlets, ads and brochures dated from 1978 to the present. Mostly the expected soft-side propaganda, but sifting through it I found this gem, a real bare-knuckle small space ad. It hadn't even made it into print, it was just a comp they tested on focus groups in 1983. Most of the test market found the ad

Fig. I.3

Typically baffling TQM diagnostic chart. This one ostensibly gives a TQM program overview.

The original concept of Right Livelihood apparently comes from the teachings of Buddha, who described it as work consciously chosen, done with full awareness and care, and leading to enlightenment.

 Marsha Sinetar

19

insulting or Tayloristic, but it got a huge response from assembly-line bosses and those who classified their management style as "adversarial." I stuck it right on the cover page of my proposal and I don't think anyone read beyond that. ↘

Re: Taylor, you may benefit from a look at his biography [The One Best Way: Frederick Winslow Taylor and the Enigma of Efficiency, by Robert Kanigel], given that many consider his private neuroses as instructive to the modern management thinker as his public, and better-known, stop-watch management efforts.

Management theory, according to the case against it, has four defects: it is constitutionally incapable of self-criticism; its terminology usually confuses rather than educates; it rarely rises above basic common sense; and it is faddish and bedeviled by contradictions that would not be allowed in more rigorous disciplines. The implication of all four charges is that management gurus are con artists, the witch doctors of our age, playing on business people's anxieties in order to sell snake oil. The gurus, many of whom have sprung suspiciously from the "great university of life" rather than any orthodox academic discipline, exist largely because people let them get away with it. Witch doctors, after all, often got it right—by luck, by instinct, or by trial and error.

REF. NO. 7) AUTHOR(S) **John Micklethwait and Adrian Wooldridge**

Welcome to the fad-surfing age, complete with a seemingly endless supply of programs and mantras for accomplishing "breakthroughs" in performance and achieving "world-class" results. To review just a few of the options: you can, if you wish, flatten your pyramid, become a horizontal organization, and eliminate hierarchy from your company. You can empower your people, open your environment, and transform your culture. You can listen to your customers, create a customer-focused organization, and commit to total customer satisfaction. You can do the "vision thing," write a mission statement, and put together a strategic plan. You can improve continuously, shift your paradigms, and become a learning organization. You can devote yourself and your company to total quality management. Or you can reengineer your corporation, with the intent, in the words of the original reengineers, of creating a "business revolution."

...Each of [these options], in fact, has value and can create good results—when carefully selected as means to achieve specific operating and performance goals and modified to meet the needs of a particular organization..... But, precisely because they are powerful management tools, they all also hold the potential for wreaking organizational havoc and causing tremendous damage, especially when they are seen as panaceas and applied blindly across a business, without attention to where they might be useful, why, with what other techniques they are being combined, and how, if at all, they should be modified to meet the needs of the company.

REF. NO. 8) *See notes, pp. 148-151* AUTHOR(S) **Eileen C. Shapiro**

[T]he most common criticism of management theory focuses on the fourth charge: its faddishness. Management theorists have a passion for permanent revolution that would have made Leon Trotsky or Mao Zedong green with envy. Theorists are forever unveiling ideas, christened with some acronym and tarted up in scientific language, which are supposed to "guarantee competitive success." A few months later, with the ideas tried out and "competitive success" still as illusory as ever, the theorists unveil some new idea. The names speak for themselves: theory Z, management by objectives, brainstorming, managerial grid, T groups, intrapreneureship, demassing, excellence, managing by walking around, and so on....

Management fashions seem to be growing ever more fickle: the life cycle of an idea has now shrunk from a decade to a year or less.

REF. NO. 9) AUTHOR(S) **John Micklethwait and Adrian Wooldridge**

21

Just what makes
that little ol' ant

Think he'll move
that rubber tree
plant

Anyone knows an ant
can't

Move a rubber tree
plant

But he's got high
hopes

He's got high hopes

He's got high apple
pie in the sky
hopes

etc.

'High Hopes,' sung
by Doris Day in 'A
Hole in the Head'

Yet if this journal is evidence of my proposal going through, it's also a reminder of the grave misstep I may or may not have made.

The idea here is that I'd had to present the Journal as a TQM continual-improvement initiative in order to sell it. So the good news was that Senior Management backed the program immediately and heartily. And when they brought me in last Monday to tell me so, that is, to 'applaud my proaction,' I made sure to keep the TQM ball rolling. I told them I was just doing my part, taking up the quality gauntlet, how I thought it was time I made my position here really count for something. I may even have made reference to that ant-and-rubber-tree song, I mean I was going for broke. And it made for five or ten minutes of great fun, sending my managers into fits with that 'results-oriented' and 'untapped productivity' talk.

But I had no idea what I'd set in motion. Words of praise for me and for the program quickly waxed hyperbolic, which was all right, but then people began rising up from their seats and drumming their fists on the table and growing strident. This was trouble. A few sparks of initiative were being fanned before my eyes into a great TQM conflagration, something I'd clearly be unable to control. I would apparently be authoring a "new quality management paradigm," I'd unwittingly set off a "bottom-up quality revolution," raised a "new quality standard" and was "clearing a path to the millennium." I found myself backed into a corner, with my Senior Managers whooping around the conference room like primitives around a fire.

Here was the bad news, then. I'd been mistaken for an employee who just couldn't get enough TQM, who'd gone out of his way to bring more TQM into his life. The thing is, I'd seen the Journal as a legitimate way to address some heavy personal issues, to start putting my career and my life into perspective. And I'd seen it as a legitimate way to take four paid days off of work. But now I'd entered into some Faustian pact with Senior Management, evidence of which would be found the next morning, on a sinister little note wedged upright on my keyboard.

After all, my managers had carried the SysCorp motion in a fit of TQM intoxication and now it was the morning after, and like misbehaving drunks they were saying we authorized WHAT? They'd since reviewed my proposal with a sober eye, and talked to SysCorp, and there was going to be some fine print. If this journal were our berth through uncharted waters of TQM, so be it; unorthodoxy they could handle, but the program sounded almost...well, enjoyable. This clearly flew in the face of TQM. It was time to retrench.

First, I'd be granted two, not four, days to compose the journal. And I'd do it in my cubicle, taking whatever phone calls came in during that time. And if that hadn't sufficiently soured the deal, there was this matter of a summation brief:

opinion that both your journal keeping, and SysCorp's considered notations, will become valuable tools for career-building. The transcription of your thoughts during the workday will not only allow you to refine or focus your thinking on the beneficial and problematic aspects of your work-life, but will provide a kind of script for your involvement in weekly TQM discussions. Further, the input you receive from SysCorp will lend perspective to these discussions—and to your own thinking—that you may not otherwise have accessed.

Yet this being our first exposure to such a process we must condition your involvement in the following ways:

6. (a) In keeping with TQM's emphasis on result quantification, you will be asked upon completion of the program to draft a summary brief, in which you will describe and defend the efficacy of the program, list the the means you've discovered to enhance your personal and group performance, and discuss the practicable 'next steps' that might allow you to implement what you've learned. We will accept this brief in lieu of the annotated journal itself, which we understand to be a confidential document. You will be free to include passages of this journal in your summary, at your discretion.

So this was the party line, my rope-enough-to-hang-myself approval. If I backed out now they'd peg my whole sales pitch for a sham. And if the TQM wheels came off further down the road, it could mean real disaster—I'd be held accountable for a $2250.00 Human Resources outlay, I'd be guilty of bastardizing TQM and duping my superiors.

On the other hand, though, if I could keep the soft-shoe going, the Journal might—along with its broader personal benefits—make me a TQM superstar around here, something I could parlay into, I don't know, a raise, a transfer...?

The decider's going to be that summation brief. In which I'll need to spell out the secrets of the well-geared work engine and my happy place therein. Life, career, contentment, productivity, success each resolving, with the aid of my marked-up Journal, into its own pat, bulleted axiom. Well. In for a penny, I suppose....

23

> Sun Tzu's theory of adaptability to existing situations is an important aspect of his thought. Just as water adapts itself to the conformation of the ground, so in war one must be flexible; he must often adapt his tactics to the enemy situation. This is not in any sense a passive concept, for if the enemy is given enough rope he will frequently hang himself. Under certain conditions one yields a city, sacrifices a portion of his force, or gives up ground in order to gain a more valuable objective. Such yielding therefore masks a deeper purpose, and is but another aspect of the intellectual pliancy which distinguishes the expert in war.

REF. NO. _10_)   AUTHOR(S)   **Samuel Griffith, on Sun Tzu**

9:52 AM -- Back to it

Price check, job status check, new job entry, company info, blame allocation for a botched job. These are the five types of business-related calls I get, in endless repetition and in only slightly varied form, all day. "Hi, this is Mark...?" "Hi, this is Mark...?" I carol my greeting an average of 53 times a day into the receiver. What comes after that is the reason for this journal.

We're a service bureau, or prepress house. We take in electronic files from designers and output them as color prints or slides or analog film. The men and women who actually do the work here are well-equipped to run the machines of production, but they're not a reliably charming bunch. In fact, it was a second shift drum-scanner who birthed the CS team in 1987, by swatting a client in the ear with his calipers.

So out came customer service, an incorrigibly upbeat gang of college-educated lackeys, wet-nurses and punching bags, a new public vanguard for the company that's growing hell-for-leather into the millennium. Only by special arrangement now will a client speak directly to a production staffer or a group manager; otherwise a CS rep is your lone point of contact. Need to open an account, from your car phone, while you chew a wad of gum with your front teeth? Feeling ignored or trod upon, on the receiving end of too many tantrums, thinking you'd like to have a tantrum of your own? How about running those

Fig. 1.4

No. 50 Binder Clip Finger Puppet Theater

1. Hold binder clip b/w thumb and middle finger

2. Press firmly enough to leave impression on finger

3. Brace for hilarity

Mssr. Poppet: "Allo! Je suis ta nouvelle marionette des doigts. Je suis içi pour passer du temps amusant avec toi!"

jokes of yours past someone who's sure to get a bang out of them?
Whenever you'd like your opinions seconded, your mistakes laughed off,
your professional and intellectual authority--eminence--lustily sworn to,
you've got a customer service professional here who's paid to stay on
the line with you.

I'm waiting by the phone with my price lists, my prepress and software
manuals, and a job-status spreadsheet called the 'tracker' on my monitor.
I'm waiting with great stores of humility, patience and zeal. But mostly
I'm just waiting, as it happens. Time passes here like it probably does
for policemen and firemen, meaning glacially, until a little bell sounds
and everyone goes ass-over-elbows. I look forward to the crisis calls
like a fireman might look forward to struggling through a burning hotel.
And as for the boring ones, well, they're boring. Basically there aren't
any fun phone calls, only different degrees of non-fun:

9:52. Are we open 24 hours? Yes we are. Except on Sundays we're
open (click) from noon to 6.

9:55; 9:57. Fifteen (we're not supposed to say *dollars*) is what one
letter-sized plate of film "will run a guy"; 5 tabloid color ink-jets
will run that same guy 55.

10:00. Certainly, heading in from the North? Driving? You'd take 93
south to the Kennedy Parkway, and basically you're going clockwise
around Morrow Square because they're all one-way streets, until you hit
Congress--well it's not as complicated as it sounds, of course--okay by
subway it's the C line to Morrow, you'll either come out in the lobby
of the building across the street--Congress Street--
parking? Sure it's all metered parking and there's a
municipal lot next to the post office.

(Whump, whump...whump goes the AC unit like some
great lumbering animal. They just refitted the fan
this winter but it's already gone eccentric again.
Christ do those people suck, sez Jason Pitcher to no
one in particular.)

10:03. Receiver goes off in my ear like a fire-
cracker. Stan Mason ordered COLOR scans and he's
looking at them RIGHT now and they're ALL GREYSCALE
(see 10:17, though) and I've apparently got a BIG
problem on my hands. Pal. Well I give that talk
right back to him: "Let's try to be civil here,
pal"--yeah we'll see who's the pal, pal. Stan makes
a gurgling-type noise, and then he recaps: "This is
a BIG problem, Mark, and I'm holding YOU responsible, and it's, you'd damn well better find out how
to solve it and call me RIGHT back" (fumble and

A word on
the score:

This is the
film-montage
part of
"Barbs on
the Wire: The
Mark Thornton
Story" where
you'd hear
Alice Cooper
doing "Wel-
come to my
Nightmare."

click). I wonder, not for the first time, what would have drawn a guy who cringes from conflict into the field of customer service.

(A band of heat swims up from behind my monitor, a ceiling light dips into a shallow arc and rights itself. *Bonk!* time to get crowned by Rattner's orange. My teeth grit down hard.).

10:06. You can get a letter-size Matchprint for 65. Now beat it.

10:16. An otherwise good guy from MacroSys has to call and "light a fire" under me, while the manager who's put him up to it hangs in earshot. Pawns and kings in every company I guess.

(You're watching TV? Maria screeching into her phone, Oh my god I hate you. Kendra's telling Desmond about a tick that fell down the back of her shirt on Martha's Vineyard.)

10:17. Wait 'til I get a load of this. Those scans are fine, yeah they're in color all right. It's just that Stan--heh--only started using his new monitor this morning, and it's a black and white model, which he hadn't realized. It shows everything in greys, even color scans, which they indeed are! Sorry about the hot-flash there but, well I've got to admit it's one hilarious mixup.

Yes I do, I do have to admit that, it's a requirement of the job. Like talking caffeine-addled art directors down from every window ledge in the city, like delving through a Congo of paper and electronic records after jobs no one's even heard rumor of, mugging and coddling and stretching my neck across the chopping block for every viperous half-wit sucker who can dial our number--

10:20. "Good morning, it's John Hayward at FirstStep?" Okay, FirstStep: makers of Soft and Gentle-brand infant toys, who can't even bear to use hard consonants in the product name: 'Soff n' Gennle.' The staff there is anything but, more like Cheap n' Cantankerous.

"Morning, John, what can I do for you?"

"Well, since you ask (he stifles a laugh), I called in reference to an invoice I just got, number 135 double-0 six, the P.O. was SNG1015. You've got that information there, don't you?"

"One moment, uh-yes, that's a bill we sent out from receivables in June, for work done on 5.30, that right?"

"That's the one, Mr. Mark." John's just bursting with phony good cheer this morning.

"Alright, what's the--"

"Anyway, there's a charge here for 16 dylux proofs and we only ordered 4, and received 4? And I'd like to be credited for the difference."

"Sure, let me look through that, ah-but it looks like we burned 16 plates of film into four proofs, and we charge by the burn so it'd be the same as 16 single-plate proofs. Is this making sense?"

"Does it make sense? Let's see...<u>no</u> it does *not* make sense. And I'll caution you against taking that tone with me. I'm <u>not</u> some idiot five-year-old. And I didn't call to argue with you today, sir."

"Well sure you didn't, of course not. And I'm—"

"So let me just, if you'll let me talk, if you'll let the client get a word in, would you mind please putting me through to your manager? No need to waste any more of your time, or mine, I can see where this is going. I'll take this up with your manager, thank you."

"Sure John, but he's only going to give you the same story..."

"Na-aturally. You'd better put me through all the same though, thanks, unless you want me to call him direct?"

"Nope, here you go."

Fine. I punch 'transfer' and dial for Lon, who picks up on the third ring. He's got me on speaker and sounds like he's fallen into a well.

"Thornton. What's on your mind."

"Sorry, Lon, I've got John Hayward from FirstStep, he's getting out of hand here, he's decided he needs to go over my head."

"—lem now?" I can hear the springs working in his chair.

"Sorry?"

"I said 'what's he want?'"

"He's arguing a bill, we sent him four dyluxes and charged him—"

"—to repeat that first part?"

"I said he's arguing a bill for four dyluxes"—basically yelling now—"each one was a 4-plate proof, and we charged him, you know, for six<u>teen</u>, but he doesn't get it."

Lon's creased because he might actually have to do some customer service. "Mark, these aren't the kinds of things I should have landing on my plate. Our pricing is straightforward enough—"

"No, I know—"

"—"

"I'm sorry, go ahead."

"Thornton." Lon fully exasperated. "You're keeping a client on the line. Which means you're making him even more angry. You're going to have to put him through and—"

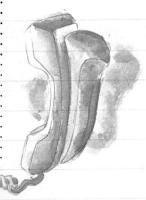

Fig. I.5

Shoulder prop on phone receiver. These are not standard issue—got mine from a guy in scanning who was about to toss his out.

27

In the Vale of the Despots:
A Select Inventory of
Management Office
Furnishings

— First thing you see in
Lon's office is the poster
over his bookcase, a huge
likeness of Yosemite Sam,
his pistols drawn and
smoking, and floating
above him the word
Welcome. Mixed message!

— Clay Pirner's wastebasket
is an upended Uncle Sam
Hat. He's said to have
welded and painted it himself, and to have "moved"
similar "units" to
friends.

— Also in Clay's office, a
Jack LaLanne Juice Tiger
for brewing fruit drinks
and mixing vitamin power-
shakes.

— Karen Fendi: 10 tins of
albacore tuna in pyramid
arrangement on credenza
(See fig. I.6)

— SVP, Marketing:
Framed still from
the movie Samson
and Delilah:
Samson (Victor
Mature) has
been shorn and
blinded and, to
the delight of Roman
onlookers, is being
marauded by a troupe of
midgets. Caption reads:
Don't Let the Bastards
Get You Down.

"Fine," I say, knowing the speaker will
clip me out. I can either hit 'transfer' again
or hang up to patch the client in, but I
shield the receiver and hit 'conference.' Lon's
still talking:

"—on through, what's the name again?...Hello?"

"Hello, is this Lon Baffert?"

Some kind of scuffle breaks out in Lon's
office. Off goes the can-and-thread-phone sound
of the speaker, and Lon recovers in his client
voice. Might be Lon in there or George Reeves.

"—ah, yeahs, problem with the phones, sorry.
So this would be John from FirstStep?"

"It would: hi Lon. Hoping you can help me
with something."

"Very good, let's talk. How can I make you
happy today?"

"I'll tell you, Lon, I call in a simple query
on a bill, and next thing I know I'm getting this
terrific hassle from a young man on your staff—
well, from someone I won't name just now." Me?

"Tell me what to do to make it right, John."

"Hah. Good. Anyhow, so I've got this young
man, Lon, explaining away a 75-dollar over-
charge before he's even had a look at the job.
And then he won't put me through to you, sup-
posably (sic) you're just going to parrot what
he said to me, he seemed to feel pretty certain about that."

"What can I say, John. We do our best to
train these guys, but they're out there on their
own. Between you and me though, I know who the
young man in question is, and he's about to get
a serious mano-a-mano when we hang up."

"Oh now I don't think—" John begins,
inconcealably pleased.

"—no, that's my decision. Now, with our
bills here we say nothing gets writ in stone.
Accounting's going to review your job. You may
get the same total again, but in the meantime
you'll have bought another 30 days to pay it.
How does that sound?" Replacing my receiver,
gingerly, in its cradle.

Listening

- Affirming with words like:
  -- "Really?"
  -- "Uh-huh."
  -- "I see."
  -- "Sure."

- Bridging by tying what the speaker just said to some related part of the topic. Examples include:
  -- "As you mentioned earlier..."
  -- "That reminds me to ask you..."
  -- "I'd like to follow up on..."

- Organizing. Prepare to listen by:
  -- putting unrelated materials aside
  -- sitting in a location comfortable for listening
  -- arranging to avoid interruptions

- Confirming
  -- State what you understood.
  -- Check that the statement is correct. For example:
    - "Is that correct?"
    - "Is that it?"
    - "Right?"

Building Rapport

- Build rapport
  -- Use common courtesy
  -- Make personal connection, such as sharing your own experience that was similar to the point being discussed
  -- Use team language, such as we, our, let's, together, we can.
  -- Display positive facial and body language, such as nodding, frequent eye contact, and smiling.
  -- Acknowledge that you hear and understand other people's points of view, even when you do not agree with them.

- Avoid Undermining Rapport with:
  -- rudeness
  -- inappropriate tone of voice, such as curtness or condescension
  -- inaccuracy
  -- demanding jargon, such as "you must" or "we must"
  -- technical jargon

REF. NO. 11) *See notes, pp. 148-151*   **AUTHOR(S)**   **Juran Institute**

Begin master-minding your own business conversations today!

- - - - - - - - - - - -

THE EMPTY BOAT

If a man is crossing a river
And an empty boat collides with his own skiff,
Even though he be a bad-tempered man
He will not become very angry.
But if he sees a man in the boat,
He will shout at him to steer clear.
If the shout is not heard, he will shout again,
And yet again, and begin cursing.
And all because there is somebody in the boat.
Yet if the boat were empty,
He would not be shouting, and not angry.

If you can empty your own boat
Crossing the river of the world,
No one will oppose you,
No one will seek to harm you.

REF. NO. 12)   **AUTHOR(S)**   **Thomas Merton, after Chuang-tzu**

An Eastern-flavored approach for what ails.

10:26 AM -- Inexplicable behavior

Lon comes barreling out of his office like some lunatic escapee and with no kind of introduction at all it's time to 'get psyched.' He races around the whole group, starting with Rattner:

"Rattner!" The noise makes everyone start. "Lon?" "Get psyched, Rattner!" "Okay."

"Maria, you psyched?"

"Yes."

"Thornton--"

"--I'm psyched!--"

"--get psyched! Shannahan!"

"Hey Lon!"

"Get psyched!...eh, what?"

"Are you psyched?"

"'Course I'm psyched, look at me!"

"I like it, Lon!"

"Tunney! Where's Tunney?"

"Getting coffee. We'll ask her when she gets back. Ah-but she looked psyched."

"I like it! Ritchie!"

"Yeah Lon?"

"Get psyched, Ritchie!"

And so on, all the way around the group. I can't imagine him not jogging right back to his office and making an entry in his management journal: "10:25--Unannounced morale check. Really fired them up good." Hey, you don't get to be a bridge facilitator for Jay Gathers without being somewhat resourceful....

Managers focus so earnestly on "positive" values—employee satisfaction, upbeat attitude, high morale—that it would strike them as destructive to make demands on employee self-awareness. Yet employees dig deeper and harder into the truth when the task of scrutinizing the organization includes looking at their own roles, responsibilities, and potential contributions to corrective action.

| REF. NO. 13 | See notes, pp. 148-151 | AUTHOR(S) | **Chris Argyris** |

HOW TO MOTIVATE GENERATION X

➤ Make training an obsession in your organization. Fill the workplace with training resources.

➤ Teach Generation X workers to micromanage themselves. Help them carve up the job into bite-size chunks so they can see the day-to-day results.

➤ Move from six-month or 12-month reviews to frequent, accurate, specific and timely feedback.

➤ Reward people daily for stellar performance. Extend menu of nonfinancial incentives.

| REF. NO. 14 | See notes, pp. 148-151 | AUTHOR(S) | **Rainmaker, Inc.** |

From a USA Today article. These are the kinds of titles your managers are taking very seriously.

30

10:27 AM -- Archetypes of the American Workplace: Put-upon Overachiever Karen Fendi

If someone were to fire a cannonball past CS this morning I'd see more of it than I do Karen Fendi. "Hello hello hello" she's saying, bolting toward her office, coffee held out in front of her like a relay baton. Rattner makes the *Ree-ow!* sound of a racecar speeding past and Karen returns more hello's--Hello CS! Hello! punctuated with the slam of her office door. Between her excursions and Lon's, it's like the tolling of a pair of cuckoo clocks.

Our dealings with Karen are all but restricted to these scissor-legged fly-by's. You wouldn't see those tiny and severe lineaments of hers or their iron-colored outlines and underscores, those powder-burn freckles, that Einsteinian disregard for her hair, those sensibly-matched blouses and long skirts, you might not have any idea what she looked like unless you'd cornered her in her office. Karen's working when I get in and she's working when I leave; there are no exceptions to this. If she transacts any kind of personal life, no one in this corporation is privy to it. Whether she leaves the building at all, in fact, is a secret of third shift and the cleaning crews. And what's the payoff for Karen? Well, for starters, she's able to excite a great deal of concern for her in her coworkers, so she gets to hear, and quite often: Karen you've <u>got</u> to take a break or you're just going to <u>burn out</u>. Want to win her friendship? Tell her she's courting a major breakdown, it's that simple. Then she'll get to say, voice all a-flutter "Oh I appreciate it but I...I just don't know..." as her eyes lose focus and start wandering some empty corner of the ceiling, her expression becoming suddenly pious.

I feel the need to unsettle Karen. In a helpful way, I mean. Make her jump the rails, have her look objectively at how she's managing herself and where she's headed, at how martyrdom tends to work out for the martyr. Our conversations usually end up like psychoanalytic interviews, which is why she keeps them brief. Like when I'd learned about her vacation to Japan and was pressing her about that:

Tell me, I'd asked her, how you were finally able to leave work? (Not that I didn't already know, I just wanted to hear her explain.)

Fig. I.6

Pyramid arrangement of albacore tuna tins on Fendi's credenza

Karen: Well it was suggested, firmly suggested, that I take a break.

Me: But everyone tells you to take time off. You love it. You get to say 'I will, I will,' with the understanding that you never would.

Karen: (Laughs) Ah-no, this is...this was different. The request came down, formally, from Senior Management. If you take my meaning. The incident, I'm not sure if you were here yet, but it was just before they changed file servers, actually it was why they had to, where all those files were being lost and some virus, or something had just ravaged the accounting archives, when we used to store them on 8mm DAT...?

Me: Yes, I mean no, I wasn't here but it's company legend. Don Eiden walked in on you....

Karen: Yeah, well we were having to piece the entire month together, just from paper records. And I was looking ahead to year-end, and just, you can't imagine the pressure, what kind of job that would be at year-end. So yeah, I just, I don't know why but I had my hands up like this (grips the hair at her temples) and I, you know, was pulling at it, hard. I remember some blood, and Don standing there. It was a while ago.

Me: So then they suggested--

Karen: No, it was after I threw my PC off my desk.

Me: Threw it? I've seen you struggle with that thing, just repositioning it....

Karen: Well it's like, some women have been known to lift cars off of their children, you know?

Me: I can see that, sure, in extremis.

Karen: Well this was, for me. I was beyond extremis. It was the Friday of that week with the hair-pulling deal. I'd struggled all day with a spreadsheet file that refused to open, something they guaranteed me had not corrupted. My machine must have crashed a dozen times and, you know, I'd had enough.

(stands to enact the following, weird quizzical look on her face) I picked it up and, I turned maybe a quarter of the way around and just sort of dropped it--*pschhew*. (sits) They were able to fix it, no problem, you know, just cosmetic damage, but the crash was enormous. I had a memo on my desk from Senior Management before the damn thing hit the ground.

Me: And is this, you'd describe this as a healthy reaction to stress?

Karen: Healthy? That isn't a word that...races to mind. No, more like a petit mal or something, like apoplexy. I don't spend too much time looking back at that. I feel like too much self-examination, in my case anyway, it isn't such a hot idea (appends a nervous laugh).

Here's where I backed off, I mean Karen _is_ a middle manager. But if I'd finished the thought--

No, but you need, you <u>cultivate</u> concern for you in others, you need us there warning you about a breakdown, just reminding you we know how doggedly you're pursuing one. Is that validating for you, that kind of concern?

Karen: What? Do I feel validated when people tell me I'm sinking my life into my job? Well, I think I feel more remorse, or like I want to tell them that I <u>do</u> have a personal life, like this isn't all I do, accounting. But inasmuch as they recognize the contribution I make, the hours I put in, sure it's validating. That might not be the exact word I'd use, that's your word. But yeah.

Me: Sure, although who really knows what you're up to in accounting, right, aside from the accountants? For the rest of us it's all inference, and if we imagine you're making a big contribution it's only because of the way you act, right? So that's why it's the injured athlete routine with you, the soldier knee-deep in a mantrap: No no, mustn't worry about me, you people carry on. It's the image you've made for yourself and that you're doomed to maintain now, Karen Fendi giving recklessly and perpetually and without stint to the corporation--that's the facade and then beyond it, and just as important, there's that inner frailty, the helplessness you'll hint at and then

Fig. I.7
"Cosmetic damage" to Karen's monitor.

refuse to admit to. Because we're meant to observe it, that
frailty, but not to interfere, that's the element you need to
preserve so that if you can't win respect, you can settle for
compassion...?

   Karen: Wow, umm, I don't know about that. I generally don't
think in those terms. I don't know what to say to that--actual-
ly, is this going to take much longer, by the way? There are
some new business accounts that, well, they're not going to
administer themselves....

People tend to see their work and personal lives as separate spheres. While they recognize the
conflicts between these spheres, they usually see them as their private responsibility to manage
and contain.... In probing deeper...some of the cultural assumptions that drive the work begin to
surface, and people start to talk about how emergencies are glorified and the people who respond
to them are seen as heroes, how staying late is a way to show you care about the work, how solving
crises is rewarded while preventing them is not, or how a willingness to sacrifice personal time sig-
nals commitment.

REF. NO. *15*   )   *See notes, pp. 148-151*   AUTHOR(S)   **Lotte Bailyn et al.**

. . . .

Ironically, most people who work experience a more enjoyable state of mind on the job than at
home. At work it is usually clear what needs to be done, and there is clear information about how
well one is doing. Yet few people would willingly work more and have less free, leisure time. Those
who do are pitied as "workaholics." Generally unnoticed is the fact that the work we want to avoid is
actually more satisfying than the free time we try to get more of.

REF. NO. *16*   )   *See notes, pp. 148-151*   AUTHOR(S)   **Mihaly Csikszentmihalyi**

An inter-generational perspective on your Karen — and yes, if you're delving
into that literature, you'll have to steel yourself against the generational monikers.

Xers keep life in perspective.... Xers are the most likely to agree that they'd be willing to "work at
a boring job as long as the pay was good," and they are the least likely of all generations to describe
work as a career. It's not that they prefer boredom, rather, it's just that work is not an all-consuming
passion for them. This is a distinctive balancing of priorities. Xers want a job *and* a life. Boomers,
on the other hand—and this is something Xers see and explicitly reject—have largely seen their
jobs as their lives, a generational pursuit of self-fulfillment in the workplace.

REF. NO. *17*   )   *See notes, pp. 148-151*   AUTHOR(S)   **Yankelovich Partners, Inc.**

10:28 AM -- Electronic Mail Revue

E-mail hasn't yet won a company-wide embrace, though we've been hooked up for nearly two years. What it's done instead is marginalize a stubborn minority of traditionalists, who aren't content just to stay off the network, they need for it to be dismantled. On the plus side, the issue has allowed company cranks, oddballs and sociopaths to forge some new friendships. They stump-preach about entropy, the depersonalization of communications, the propagation of armchair culture, the invitation for everyone to access everyone else immediately and with all manner of nonsense, &c. Half the holdouts are just lazy and reactionary technophobes, the kind who panic any time their skill set threatens to expand. The rest are diehard Luddites for whom it's become a pitched ideological battle and, you know, good for them.

For high strung self-editors like me, though, it's glorious, that non-immediacy of e-mail. After stammering my way through the 10-10:30 fusillade of client calls, I get to compose and deliver my statements as deliberately as you'd move chess pieces. It's what I've always dreamt of doing in conversation, really, freezing the action, mulling my options, and parrying with my cleverest material, such as it is.

And I get to strain out any inflection that could undercut or misdirect what I'm trying to say. Here I am writing to Paul Slaney, who's just asked me to show up here at 8:30 on Sunday morning for his recycling drive: "8:30--Yikes! Really, it's no sweat. I'll be up and about then anyway, glad to pitch in." Glad, at 8:30, on Sunday? Sure, there it is in writing, I almost believe it myself.

Next up, Lon reminds us of a 10:45 emergency TQM session in the small conference room near reception. And he re-reminds us of Jay Gathers' engagement here this evening. That Lon puts the 'b' in subtle, all right. Yes, we know we've got to get our act together if we're to be worthy of Dr. Gathers' attentions. And yes, we who've ranged farthest from the path will be the first penitents at his hem, humbly awaiting receipt of the Word and now who's got an a-men?

A flicker of hope arrives next, in the form of Rebby Conlon's public posting: the design group has opened up the Corporate Challenge 5K t-shirt contest. This year Rebby, the Creative Director up there, will take design submissions from anyone in the company. Doubt they'd consider a photographic approach, but

Fig. I.8

Scar shaped
like square-
root symbol
on heel of
my right
hand. Got it doing a
Mary Poppins routine, at
sister's behest, off of
garage roof. What am I
doing right now? Why,
I'm sitting in my cube
and staring at my hand.

you can silk-screen a photo onto
fabric as easily as anything else.
When our squad runs the race we all
wear the t-shirt and awards are
given for best design, best use of
corp. identity, etc. Who knows? The
odds are long that (a) I'll pull
something together in time, (b) that
one of these yahoos won't better
render that corporate *je ne sais
quoi*, which is still one of my
life's great mysteries, and (c) that
one sweat-streaked photo on a sin-
gle-use t-shirt will give my career
much of a boost, award or no. Still,
Rebby's call for entries is as
pleasant an introduction to midmorn-
ing as I'm likely to get.

THE GOLDEN EAGLE

A man found an eagle's egg and put it in the nest of a backyard hen. The eaglet hatched with the brood of chicks and grew up with them.

All his life the eagle did what the backyard chickens did, thinking he was a backyard chicken. He scratched the earth for worms and insects. He clucked and cackled. And he would thrash his wings and fly a few feet into the air.

Years passed and the eagle grew very old. One day he saw a magnificent bird far above him in the cloudless sky. It glided in graceful majesty among the powerful wind currents, with scarcely a beat of its strong golden wings.

The old eagle looked up in awe. "Who's that?" he asked.

"That's the eagle, the king of the birds," said his neighbor. "He belongs to the sky. We belong to the earth—we're chickens."

So the eagle lived and died a chicken, for that's what he thought he was.

REF. NO. 19) —— adapted from the original by Anthony de Mello

. . . .

Do something, it matters little or not at all whether it be in the way of what you call your profession or not, so it be in the plane or coincident with the axis of your character.

REF. NO. 20) *See notes, pp. 148-151* AUTHOR(S) Ralph Waldo Emerson

10:35 AM -- Elevator to High Comedy

After a visit to Nelson in the downstairs patisserie, I'm holding an elevator door for Paul Varela, one of two bicycle couriers we keep on staff. A gem of a mid-summer day shaping up outside but I resist saying: "Great day to be a courier, hah?" because he'd have to shoot back "Every day's a great day to be a courier." He steps in, hits floor 10 and asks if I'm ready.

"Wha? Paul, I got a full cup of coffee in my hand." Holding it up to prove this.

"Drink some off," he sez. I try, and get the roof of my mouth scalded for it. "Paul?"

"You ready, you ready?" he's repeating, watching the floor numbers light up. 3, 4, 5. Paul's going to show me how he can stop the car on 9 without punching the 9 button. "Better drink some off, better drink some off, can't blame me." 6, 7. The idea is that if you jostle the car mightily enough it'll freeze anywhere. Then just hit door-open and step out. It's a question of timing, a knack he's supposed to have though I know he just as often traps himself between floors, sometimes with passengers and sometimes for an hour or more. I pluck open the emergency phone box, casual as you please. Nothing in there but somebody's popsicle stick.

We pass the 8th floor and he pauses for a beat, grabs the handrail and starts shaking at it like it's carrying a lethal current. My coffee goes sloshing all over the rim, I'm dodging it as expertly as I can and trying to keep my balance with the whole works shaking like a paint mixer. We do stop, though, and the doors do open to our floor, give or take. A step up of about 2 feet. The Hollies in reception watch us climb out and are amused.

Shaking coffee off my knuckles now, but I've managed to spare my shirt. "Son of a <u>bitch</u>" is all I've got for Paul, who goes clomping back to shipping in his bike shoes.

Fig. I.9: Paul Varela's left ear.

Of particular interest is the lobe-stretcher now in vogue among alternative-nation trendmongers. Looks painful but Paul sez he doesn't even notice it. He will when he's somebody's grandfather and he's still got earlobes like a Ubangi.

Gretchen, whose last name she informs me is unimportant, is slumming with us again today. She freelances for the design group, where they're overrun with work and bodies but not so with machines. Which sends a little diaspora of temps and low-ranking staffers to the far corners of the company, there to fend for themselves in creative Siberia. A likely destination for castoffs is the work area right behind me (see CS map).

Gretchen has taken the desk nearer to the utility closet, meaning her back is about one giant step from mine. The monitor there is of course too small and not at all like the ones she's grown accustomed to at the 'bigger agencies' here and in New York, with whom her dealings have been extensive. And is she supposed to lug her own supplies into work every day? because they can <u>forget</u> that. The last speaker they had at the AIGA sucked and the banquet was a bore, and in lieu of lunch today she's brought a pack of ginseng chewing gum and if anyone would like some, it's said to be a powerful aphrodisiac. She's used to prattling on like this to keep her right brain active, so just excuse her.

Had she been told about Ann Chesney, how Ann got stuck at that same workstation?

"Hmm?"

"Ann Chesney, a Senior Manager with us from the late '80's to a couple years ago, they put her at that desk until she quit."

"I see, well gawd forbid any one of you on salary would have to work at a <u>temp</u> station," turning at last to face me, though her eyes linger on her monitor.

"That's not what I meant. The story is, Ann had put a sign up in her office window, facing out: Help me, I'm being held hostage. Someone called in a SWAT team, right? and they had to evacuate the building, cost the city $100,000. What a panic. So they decided no more windows for Ann, they made her work in that cube until she quit."

"Well I'm sure it didn't take long, no offense but it's insufferable, working in these cubes."

"That's okay I didn't build 'em. Did you know that there are even temp surgeons now?"

"Which is supposed to mean...what?"

"Dunno, it was just something I heard. And which may or may not be true."

"No--it's Mark, mmh?--no, I wasn't aware

Fig. I.10

Designer Couture lesson 1:

Gretchen's modster specs

- crimped-foil trim
- precious and semi-precious stone inlay

of that, but if you mean, well but you wouldn't mean the temp is less reliable, or a lower grade of—"

"No, I've temped as much as—"

"But if you're saying the whole economy's going temp, you're smart, I agree. Think about it." Now I've got her undivided attention. "It makes sense for managers and owners to have virtual staffs now, just salary a little skeleton shift, hire up and scale down overnight. For them it's perfect. It's perfect for us, people like me anyway, I mean I get the work whenever I want it, but I never have to put in more than I'm willing to on any given day...."

Here we go. I'm uncorking another temp-worker manifesto. Most temps aren't with us long enough to get their parking validated, but they all find time for one of these. Usually it's the 'What Are You Looking At' variety, to wit: while you're looking sidelong at me like my life must be some kind of shambles, you should be asking yourself just how secure your <u>own</u> job is because what you don't know, mister, is that corporate governors and temp agencies are deep in bed and one way or another everyone's job is going temp and we'll see who's acting so goddamned smug then, heh, when they offer up <u>your</u> job, &c.

Gretchen forgoes this for the 'Couldn't Be Happier,' which states broadly that full-time jobs are for suckers, that work is a cruel and mostly-avoidable necessity, that a 9 to 5 indenture is no substitute for a life and you'd know that if you hadn't already bought your bill of goods from the Man. Alternately the temp <u>does</u> want a full-time position, but only one that s/he can accept in its every particular, for this is a life that cannot know compromise.

Anyhow, if our temps talk about anything beyond temping you won't hear it from Gretchen. She can't get enough of my own temp-job horror stories either, so I'm reeling one off after another until Pitcher comes to collect me for our meeting. Her farewell turns out to be an elaborate one, as she may not (in fact, won't) be here when I get back. And I admit to being a little saddened until she says, tremendously, to spare her my pity, that this is how it really must be....

Fig. I.11
Got stuck in one of these concentric-cylinder revolving doors once while I was temping. Couldn't see the breach b/c I was faced the wrong way, into the darkroom I was trying to leave. Panicked after 10 min's and knocked on the wall until an art director fed the inner door around, yanked me out and sent me home.

All told, companies shelled out $4.9 billion to temps in 1995, more than double what they paid just four years earlier, according to the National Association of Temporary and Staffing Services.

REF. NO. 21) *See notes, pp. 148-151* AUTHOR(S) **The Wall Street Journal**

· · · · · · · · · · · · · · · · · ·

One really great thing that has come out of all this is that I've been cured of a certain kind of envy. I used to think it might be really great to have a wicked high-paying job and make a ton of money. Not anymore.... You know I'm not religious, but the word "Godless" springs to mind. I'll take my rice and beans, my 10 minute subway ride, and my roach infested Hell's Kitchen apartment any day. I wouldn't live like those people for all the money in the world.

REF. NO. 22) *See notes, pp. 148-151* AUTHOR(S) **Leah Ryan**

Corporations once built to last like pyramids are now more like tents. Tomorrow they're gone or in turmoil.... You can't design your life around a temporary organization.... The stepladder is gone, and there's not even the implied structure of an industry's rope ladder. It's more like vines, and you bring your own machete. You don't know what you'll be doing next, or whether you'll work in a private office or one big amphitheater or even out of your home. You have to take responsibility for knowing yourself, so you can find the right jobs as you develop and as your family becomes a factor in your values and choices.... It is time to give up thinking of jobs or career paths as we once did and think in terms of taking on assignments one after the other.

REF. NO. 23) *See notes, pp. 148-151* AUTHOR(S) **Peter Drucker**

· · · · · · · · · · · · · · · · · ·

These are the people who, by choice or circumstance, find themselves on the outside of corporate enterprise, working in. I call them portfolio people. What I mean by this I can best explain by repeating what I told my own children when they left college. "I hope you won't go looking for a job," I said. I was not advocating the indolent life or a marginal one. What I meant was that rather than scurrying about looking for a corporate ladder to climb or a professional trajectory to follow, they ought to develop a product, skill, or service, assemble a portfolio that illustrates these assets, and then go out and find customers for them....

This new notion of career is already catching on. The PR person, the marketing expert, even the project engineer and sales manager, are coming to see themselves somewhat as actors do, looking for good parts in new productions and not expecting or wanting any one part to run forever. Organizations, on their side, will have to offer a continuing series of good roles if they want to keep their best people. A promise of medical insurance will not be enough for the best of the portfolio careerists. They will want challenge and a chance to develop in their professional fields, as well as money, and they will move to wherever they can find these opportunities.

REF. NO. 24) *See notes, pp. 148-151* AUTHOR(S) **Charles Handy**

Ryan writing in a 'zine called "Temp Slave."

The Drucker and Handy readings suggest a link between the spread of temp culture and a general decline of security or permanence in the organization; what interests us is that this decline seems itself an outgrowth, or at least an

40 *emblem, of a society-wide multiplication of uncertainties. See sociological angle on pp. 116-117.*

[I]n the New People Partnership, the company assumes responsibility for investing in the employee and providing work that makes the individual "employable" in the marketplace. The employee owns his or her career and takes on the burden of building the capabilities that add value to the organization and insure his or her own marketability. The employee and the company work together to insure that the organization meets market needs and is successful, since ongoing success provides the context for ongoing employment....

For employability to work effectively, employees must actively seek and create their own career opportunities. They need to communicate openly about personal and professional needs and expectations. And they must be afforded unrestricted access to alternative job opportunities in the company.

What does this mean for the company? For one thing, it must support employees in identifying and evaluating job opportunities inside and outside the company, helping them to build a customized career path. In this environment, there is no stigma attached to looking for a new job, there is limited ownership of people except in cases of critical skills and there is a recognition that employability and managing careers are in the best interest of both the corporation and the individual. This is about a mutual investment that creates real barriers to separation, and it is about genuine trust in each other.

| REF. NO. 25) | AUTHOR(S) | **Bruce Pasternack et al.** |

Here's a management system that seems to be working for clients like Intel and 3Com and Raychem, designed around the perceived career needs of the new professional.

10:45 AM -- TQM, Live from Lon Baffert's House of Crazy!

Off now to Lon's TQM fire drill. I've got to say he revels in this. Don't know how deep his affection for the program runs, but I do know he likes time off from his administrative post--I mean for all his quirks he doesn't maintain that of actually liking his job. And then you figure he gets the pulpit in front of a captive assembly of juniors, I mean it's a marvel we're not at it all day. The uselessness of it all, the kowtowing to Senior Management, the professorial manner he's allowed to adopt--all cater to his professional 'likes.' And the aggravation it causes me is exquisite, which I have to think is another motivator for Lon.

The idea in these meetings is to deconstruct communication barriers, to collapse the tiers of authority and foster a free exchange of ideas. Simple group-based decision making, goal creation and problem resolution. Seems harmless enough, even worthwhile.

And if it were practiced as originally conceived, TQM might even deliver on some of that horizontality and free-wheeling communication. But as with any new policy rashly adopted and imperfectly understood, it trickles down to us in as many different forms as there are managers. In our case, Lon's practicing TQM like Colonel Kurtz waged his war in Vietnam.

"(Kurtz is) out there operating without any decent restraint. Totally beyond the pale of any acceptable human conduct. And he is still in the field commanding his troops."

— General Korman in 'Apocalypse Now'

41

Today we find him waiting for us in the smaller of two employee meeting rooms, this one equipped with a guttered dry-erase board and two hanging graph-paper pads all cased in a dartboard-style cabinet, flanked by a pair of flip-chart easels, with an overhead projector stashed in a corner. Definitely a place furnished for relaxed and honest communication. A "spread" on the credenza includes a kind of pie-chart arrangement of broccoli, cauliflower, peppers, celery and carrots under cellophane, next to a lidless bowl of bone-colored dip. At 10:45 in the morning, no one wants to touch it.

A weird set to Lon's face this morning, a deep thoughtfulness, perhaps, sharing space with the ghastly suggestion of mirth. It's as though he's been seized by an idea both brilliant and incendiary and is wondering how in God's name he should phrase it to a group of witless innocents. He's cupping his chin and drumming on his lips with a forefinger, breathing heavily, with his eyes angled toward the ceiling, his focus lost as though fastened to some celestial object. He wants to give us the heart-stopping impression that anything could happen. And I admit I have no idea what to expect. His face, as usual, is illegible.

> A true leader always keeps an element of surprise up his sleeve, which others cannot grasp but which keeps his public excited and breathless.
>
> Charles de Gaulle

There's a type of opaque personality that hides a rich mental life, I know, but Lon's is the other type. With Lon it's more a product of insecurity, animal cunning, a kind of office-survivalist thing. His inscrutability this morning is less the source of excitement than fear, and ours is the wariness of a boxer watching the feints of an adversary. It's not 'Oh boy, what's Lon up to?' it's 'Oh god, what is he doing?'

I open my notebook and begin fixing names to the doodles under the TQM 7/10 heading, last week's meeting. 'Spiral,' 'Army Tank Beset by Geometric Shapes,' 'Cross-hatch Studies I-IV,' 'Van Halen Flying-Initials Logo.' When I look up, Lon's out of his chair and pacing between the two easels. He grits his teeth and waits for the pre-meeting chatter to taper off, which of course it doesn't, so he consults his watch and kicks things off with an explosive throat-clearing.

"Now, alright, we're getting started here, first of all good morning." He snatches a dry-erase marker from the tray and brandishes it regally. "We're short on time today so let's settle in. Okay. Now, we were saying last time that many of us felt as though we were holding back in discussion, mmh? And then we identified a possible barrier to communication here, and, well, it was me. It seemed like just having an authority figure here was distancing us from our goal of frank and open communication. And I thought since we were saying that last time, that we'd try something different today."

Fig. I.12

Van Halen logo, *sine qua non* of the junior-high school notebook

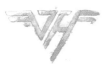

Again that weird playfulness, the air of performance. We're all hoping, after a lead-in like that, that he's just going to leave. "Soo..."—playing the marker around the room until it's leveled at Charlene—"...you, Charlene, I want you to facilitate this meeting. That's right, stand up, gather your things and bring them here and you can switch with me."

Eyes are flitting from Lon to Charlene and back. He looks the part of a parent who's opened the drapes on Christmas morning to show his dumbstruck kids a pony he's paddocked in the yard. But if we're stunned it's more like, why's he proving you don't need any special training to facilitate a TQM meeting?

Lon and Charlene actually go to the trouble of switching their effects, and then slowly and with incredible ceremony he hands over his marker. Dorothy lets fly a grand British laugh. The dry-erase marker's like our Lord of the Flies conch shell. You not only need it in order to speak, you're obligated to use it while you're speaking. We're expected to parse our thoughts into sub-thoughts, present them serially and bullet them on the dry erase board as they emerge. Again, great for natural and uninhibited communication. This morning the conch has rendered Charlene catatonic. She's just standing over Lon's old seat, her free hand stored in a back pocket, staring at her notebook like she might find some instructions there.

That Lon sure is a funny guy. He goes on rubbernecking like a rube in Charlene's chair, trying to catch anybody's eye, like "will you kids get a load of this?" This is his idea of anarchy, I think. "Um, Charlene," he prods her, gently, "why don't we pick up where we left off on Monday (spoken like 'mondie'), when we were dealing with our charter. You want to write 'Charter' down so we can get started?"

Lon will continue to conduct the meeting, of course, only from a different chair. Not that Charlene has nothing to say, she's just trying to shoehorn it all into the paper-edge bandwidth of a TQM-appropriate discussion. Though I wish she'd have come out swinging—"What do you make of this statement, Lon: we're not buying this TQM business, nobody is." Or "Why don't you take the money you're allotted for 'refreshments' this year and give it to us right now in a lump sum, like as a bonus." We could use the time to share techniques on dealing with unruly clients, or ways of evening out workload, we could orchestrate a group outing, refurnish or reorganize the CS area. But that's clearly not how it's meant to go. Instead we're carried headlong into a discussion of the customer service TQM charter.

HIERARCHY: An inevitable component of organizations that can be misunderstood and mismanaged but cannot be abolished or obliterated, even if the pyramid is flattened, de-layered, or turned on its side, or the language is tortured to prevent references to supervisors and subordinates.

Eileen C. Shapiro

43

I enjoyed one particularly meaningful synergistic experience as I worked with my associates to cre-ate the corporate mission statement for our business. Almost all members of the company went high up into the mountains where, surrounded by the magnificence of nature, we began with a first draft of what some of us considered to be an excellent mission statement.

At first the communication was respectful, careful and predictable. But as we began to talk about the various alternatives, possibilities and opportunities ahead, people became very open and authen-tic and simply started to think out loud. The mission statement agenda gave way to a collective free association, a spontaneous piggybacking of ideas. People were genuinely empathic as well as coura-geous, and we moved from mutual respect and understanding to creative synergistic communication.

Everyone could sense it. It was exciting....

The synergistic process that led to the creation of our mission statement engraved it in the hearts and minds of everyone there....

| REF. NO. *2 7* | *See notes, pp. 148-151* | AUTHOR(S) | **Stephen Covey** |

You have to under-stand that Covey is being serious here.

Now, at this point I didn't know it would turn into the greatest TQM session ever. Still seemed like an ordinary meeting in progress, the facilitator bobbing around in his chair like a cork in water, his team glazed over and slouching to all angles of inattention. I could sense an edge to Lon's enthusiasm, a kind of strain or volatility, but I was too bored to pay close attention. It might, I could have figured, have been handed down to Lon that his group wasn't toeing the TQM line, that we were one of only two teams still without a charter (design is the other), and that he'd better get us all on board before this afternoon's meeting or there'd be consequences. Hence the last-ditch team meeting, and also that confrontation we'd had this morning, which he'd certainly been put up to. But, like I say, this only becomes clear with hindsight.

Anyhow "charter" is the TQM term for a group mission statement, which in this case we had to write, output in oversized format, and post out-side the administrative offices. That's how we'd declare to the rest of the company and to any clients on tour just who we in customer service were, what values we represented, and what we'd done and would continue to do to be the very best we could be....

This is the Everest we've been plodding up for an hour now. Even

Dierdre's face is in her hands, that TQM seasickness now in full effect, Lon gaining a degree of animation to each one we lose, until we've come up with the following:

> The Customer Service Team declares it our mission to:
> -- Provide our clients with a level of service they will
>   not find elsewhere in the industry
> -- Implement a feedback mechanism, whereby client satisfac-
>   tion can be honestly assessed
>   • sources of satisfaction are isolated and reproduced,
>   individual and team performance is recognized
>   • sources of dissatisfaction are identified and
>   addressed, and what procedural changes are necessary
>   are rapidly and effectively undertaken; notice is sent
>   to all clients of any procedural changes

I don't even recall if this meant anything in its original word-ing. Charlene has done so much erasing and rewriting that our first-pass charter's looking like some kind of ransom note. Although, as an exercise in the new corporate argot, it's shaping up rather well. In true TQM fashion, any idea that threatens honesty, clarity or action gets trampled flat by the time it's put to words. We figure for this to go on indefinitely, so we're not really listening when Kendra says:

"Lon, do you think we should add something like: 'Develop focus on clearly-defined goals; conceive, test and implement actionable means to attain these goals?'"

"Abso-lutely," he trumpets, jolting some of us from stupor, "yeah, did you get that, Charlene? Just repeat that for Charlene, would you Kendra?" She does, and Lon's so fixated on the board he hasn't noticed the first crack in the dike.

There is a silence. "Anything else?" He wants to know. "Anyone?"

Dierdre perks up: "Uh, 'Act decisively on concrete issues, quanti-fy results and develop realistic metrics for success and team...eval-uation.'" She searches faces to see if we're going to pick up on this. There follows a rustling of paper, bodies squawk against chair leather. About four or five of us straighten up and begin writing.

"Right on, you guys," says Lon, in mixed elation and disbelief. "Let's keep it going...."

Rattner's the next to speak. "I think—tell me what you-all think about this. I say we post a Team Effectiveness Chart. We graph customer response on the ordinate, productivity in man-hours on the abscissa. A list of dynamic solutions are plotted in scatter-graph fashion. Then we

Heroes of the Revolution—
Kendra Shannahan

Kendra Shannahan, six-foot-three in the shade and about as stable as a pile of teacups stacked that high. Big and heedless woman. She's got seven stitches in her elbow from where she stove in a cupboard door at home. She opens her mouth, though, and out comes this little Shirley Temple voice, utterly inappropriate for a woman of that size. I'm always expecting someone to run up and thwack her on the back and have her voice drop into a more sensible register.

The only thing on Kendra's body that argues for a voice like this is that improbably small head of hers. Which only makes the package that much more arresting. Her presentation is like the old cartoon gag where one kid will climb on another's shoulders and they don some large and loose-fitting garment like a trench coat to impersonate an adult. It's as though any minute the kid on the bottom is going to peek out from Kendra's blouse.

It's amazing how many irrational, obeisant and colorless people they surround us with here. Kendra's our bulwark against the rule of the boring class.

look for groupings and trends."

A cloud passes over Lon's face, quickly, and that muscular smile returns. "Ehm, would you care to run that one down for us Mark, explain what you're getting at?"

Rattner, a year or two Lon's elder, flushes, consults his notes in an effort to stay composed. "Thought it was self-evident," he says huskily.

"Strive to attain goals."

"I think we covered that in point 3, do you see?" sez Lon.

"Then how about 'Striving toward the attaining of the goals?'"

This is glorious. I rack my brain but I'm too excited to think of anything good. There's a great deal of laughter being pent up here. Nor is Lon oblivious, exactly. He carries on with the cheerleading bit, only his excitement is betraying signs of panic. I...watch...his face stiffen into one of those sun-blasted cattle skulls you find around Death Valley, like some Georgia O'Keefe number (see p. 13 portrait). Skin scoured out and jaundiced-looking, raked tight over those long teeth....

"I've written: 'Furnish our clients with proactive solutions to concrete, um, issues?'" Dorothy trilling her r's, making mini snare-rolls of her t's. "You asking us or telling us?" Lon quips.

"How about, 'Strive for the highest benchmarks, with nothing standing in our way to be the best we can be.'"

"I just have: 'Go "All Out!"' and I put All-Out in quotes." A scattering of coughs.

"I propose a bumper sticker that says 'I'd Rather be Having a Quality Revolution,'" Desmond Ritchie sez at last, and it's like he's set off a bomb. Everyone's laughing in huge gusts and stooping for air. Chairs groan and clatter back upright, feet drum on the floor. This subsides in a great sighing, pens are taken up and notebooks drunkenly reordered, eyes are daubed, a calm follows and breaks again into laughter even more raucous.

Lon waits for as long as he can stand it, and tries to dig back out. Have to give him credit for this--the man's relentless.

When scattered titters swell into a chorus of hilarity like a nuclear chain reaction, people are acknowledging that they have all noticed the same infirmity in an exalted target. A lone insulter would have risked the reprisals of the target, but a mob of them, unambiguously in cahoots in recognizing the target's foibles, is safe.... Of course, in everyday life we don't have to overthrow tyrants or to humble kings, but we do have to undermine the pretensions of countless blowhards, blusterers, bullies, gasbags, goody-goodies, holier-than-thous, hotshots, know-it-alls, and prima donnas.

REF. NO. 28)   AUTHOR(S) **Steven Pinker**

Fig I.13: Swindell

This past weekend Swindell was pulling a t-shirt off over his head while descending a flight of stairs and the whole thing worked out rather poorly for him. Now he's got an ace bandage wrapped around his knee and a boxing-style mouse on his cheekbone

"Swindell Descending Stairs," with apologies to M. Duchamp

"Well, alright, okay enough. I think we're all a little punchy today. Maybe we've had an overdose of TQM, and there's more on the way for this evening. I--well, bet you never thought you'd be having fun in TQM, heh-heh. Okay, let's settle down. There's some important ground to cover, our topmost challenge is to complete this charter. A-and we can eat up time with jokes, which is fine with me, or we can belt this thing out. Anyone have any more jokes? No? Okay, good. Let's get 4 more points up there before we break. Let's see if we can smarten up and do our job today."

I'm beginning to think we might see a display of temper from our man Lon. Which is always exciting. At least we've burnt through that good-humored veneer. "Nothing, Mark? Charlene, you've been quiet, you want to contribute something?" Just the diffidence that might follow from a scolding.

"I've got something," says Pitcher, noticeably silent until now. His pen falls to his notepad, like a little felled tree. "Yeah, does anybody else see this as an insulting waste of time?"

Desmond Ritchie's behavior took top honors at this summer's corporate outing, with a routine that included hassling the bartender and DJ, falling into a potted palm and winging his carkeys overboard (this was a harbor cruise). His dismount was the clincher, the classic coat-room nap; lasted long enough for someone to write "Booty Nation" across his forehead in indelible ink.

All to the fiendish amusement of his coworkers, who show no signs of relenting on the jokes or the disciplinary threats even a month later. Germans call it *schadenfreude*, or the pleasure you take from the suffering of another, as in: *schadenfreude-shönste freude,* which holds that this is the purest or most desirable form of pleasure. Nor, as the behavior of Desmond's tormenters would suggest, is this a strictly German concept.

Heads snap toward Lon. We all hold our breath. A noise issues from his throat, like a click. He looks up at Jason, slowly, in the dazed and dislocated manner of someone stirred from a deep sleep. "Um," he begins, "by 'this,' do you mean TQM in general, or just this charter business?"

"Well I wasn't going to include all of TQM, but I think the argument could be made." He consults Lon's face, which is reddening to the point of ignition, and even Pitcher is forced to retrench a little. "I mean the idea behind continual improvement, I mean we all could benefit from that, I know. If we could come up with things that made sense."

I can't help tossing a little gas on the fire: "Tell him about the candle and the shotgun, Lon." But if he hears me, he doesn't let on.

"Care to, um, care to elaborate. On that thought. Jason?" Lon's visage suggesting sinister liquids on the boil.

"Well, look what we've written up there. I think people are getting punchy because none of this makes any sense. Just look at what we wrote. Can anyone explain to me what it's supposed to mean?"

Lon scans around the table once, and then again, but there's nobody to jump into the breach. This is it, I guess, Mr. Hyde time.

"God damn it!" he roars. "God, damn, it! That is it! What the—what the fuck is the matter with you people? I mean, am I supposed to think you're stupid now, is that it? A bunch of stupid, infants? Jason? Because that's how you're acting! You're going to do this <u>now</u>, you're going to <u>finish</u> it, and you're going to do it <u>now</u>." His hair's been thrown out of any sensible arrangement and he's hammering the table with his fists. His pencils and binder clips hop like items on a griddle, papers cascade to the floor unnoticed.

"Lon, you'd better watch out for your coffee," Kendra offers, genuinely afraid.

"You watch my goddamned coffee, Kendra. And Pitcher, we're going to talk. You just made a very <u>large</u> mistake, mister. Later you and me are going decide if TQM makes sense or not, we'll make sense of a <u>number</u> of things." Pitcher, brooding, fiercely attends his notebook.

"We are trying to improve this company. I am trying to make you a more effective team. I am trying to please our customers. That is our job. That is why we are paid by the owners of this company. This afternoon the managers are going to meet and make sure we're all on track. And this group is going to <u>be on track</u>. Period. Ehm, <u>period</u>."

We get right to work on that charter, all right. I'm not sure if Dr. Gathers would condone an outburst like that from a team manager, but this one serves ours <u>real</u> well. We put our shoulders to it for the next 30 minutes and come out with the required 8 points of TQM doggerel, and send it to reception to be typed and reproduced. By 12:15 we're making our way back to CS, chastened and mooning.

Still later, after lunch, Pitcher will visit each of our cubes in turn, to deliver a deadpan apology for his "indecorous conduct," this no doubt to save his job. We return the expected 'no sweat, don't worry about it, I wish I'd said it myself' &c., staring at the floor, muttering into laced fingers.

It's Lon himself who'll lift the spell. He titles his soon-to-be-famous retraction memo: <u>The CS team is not 'stupid,' as indicated in meeting.</u> Copies of which, along with uncharitable accounts of his behavior, are circulated to all points of the company. Now the whole incident will begin to achieve comedy. It's a painfully characteristic move for Lon: whatever he might have won from his outburst in terms of respect, or at least fear, he's undone again in an effort to put things right.

In the "stranger-than-fiction" category, these terms were prize winners in a "Business Jargon Competition" organized by the Financial Times and the Management Consultancies Association.

● **Horseblanket**
An overall strategic plan for business revitalization, shown on one large diagram (about the size of a horseblanket).

● **Model 'T'**
A triage group to develop a quick 'hit' system that links with the basic areas of Resource Management, Human Resources, Financial Services, and Marketing.

● **Referential Transparency**
The result of contextualization. Prospectively, a system wherein all parts are connected by a self-similar ruleset; retrospectively, that system wherein the prospective connections are observed as syntax.

Source: Gemini Consulting, Glossary of Terms.

...RSHIP SCIENCE FOR THE NEW MILLENNIUM

announcing the intensive
1-DAY MBA™

How to write your own jargon

Do you feel jealous of those who seem able to write meaningless but impressive sounding jargon with ease? Here is a simple device designed to enable anyone, no matter how lucid their natural style of writing, to turn out instant gibberish.

Thanks to Harry Harington from Fleet Street Publications for sending it in. He says he believes it was originally written by a Philip Broughton but he has no further details.

This is how the generator works: think of any three-digit number, then select the corresponding buzzword from each column. For example, 259 produces 'systematized logistical contingency'. No one will know what you are talking about but you are unlikely to be challenged.

Column 1	Column 2	Column 3
0 Integrated	0 Management	0 Options
1 Total	1 Organizational	1 Flexibility
②Systematized	2 Monitored	2 Capability
3 Parallel	3 Reciprocal	3 Mobility
4 Functional	4 Digital	4 Programming
5 Responsive	⑤Logistical	5 Concept
6 Optional	6 Transitional	6 Time-phase
7 Synchronised	7 Incremental	7 Projection
8 Compatible	8 Third-generation	8 Hardware
9 Balanced	9 Policy	⑨Contingency

There is quite a lot of scope here: the total number of phrases possible with this phrase generator is 10 x 10 x 10 = 1,000 'totally incomprehensible, meaningless obfuscations,' says Mr. Harington.

A sidebar from the same article by Andrew Gowers. Gowers writes that "[t]he distortions and indignities the winners have managed to inflict on the English language in 300 words are inspired."

The new but now familiar techniques of corporate communication—focus groups, surveys, management-by-walking-around—can block organizational learning even as they help solve certain kinds of problems. These techniques *do* help gather simple, single-loop information. But they also promote defensive reasoning by encouraging employees to believe that their proper role is to criticize management while the proper role of management is to take action and fix whatever is wrong.

Worse yet, they discourage double-loop learning, which is the process of asking questions not only about objective facts but also about the reasons and motives behind those facts.

REF. NO. 29)   *See notes, pp. 148-151*   AUTHOR(S)   **Chris Argyris**

. . . .

Creativity consultants take millions of dollars from corporations for Dilbertesque workshops on brainstorming, lateral thinking, and flow from the right side of the brain, guaranteed to turn every manager into an Edison.

Geniuses are wonks. The typical genius pays dues for at least ten years before contributing anything of lasting value. (Mozart composed symphonies at eight, but they weren't very good; his first masterwork came in the twelfth year of his career.) During the apprenticeship, geniuses immerse themselves in their genre. They absorb tens of thousands of problems and solutions, so no challenge is completely new and they can draw on a vast repertoire of motifs and strategies. They keep an eye on the competition and a finger to the wind, and are either discriminating or lucky in their choice of problems.

REF. NO. 30)   *See notes, pp. 148-151*   AUTHOR(S)   **Steven Pinker**

Construe 'genius' in this writing as the individual trying to distinguish him- or herself in the workplace (Pinker also writes that 'all of us are creative').

The message is this: that, the lucrative business of creativity consulting notwithstanding, it's not the responsibility of your managers to identify or activate your creativity. In fact, the programs designed to draw you out may have the exact opposite effect (refer back to your TQM meeting) Better prospects down the avenues of self-reliance, persistence, and simple hard work.

THE FARMER AND HIS SONS

. . . .

A rich farmer, feeling the onset of death,
Summoned his sons for a talk in private.
'Never,' he said with his remaining breath,
'Sell the heritage that is yours by birth
And was mine through my father and mother.
     Somewhere or other
A treasure lies hidden in that earth;
Where, I don't know, but in the end you'll arrive at

The right place, given some guts and toil.
When you've finished harvesting turn over your land,
Break it up, dig it, plough it, don't allow
One inch of it to escape your hand.'
The old man died, and the sons attacked the soil
So thoroughly with spade, mattock and plough
That at the year's end every field
     Gave them a bigger yield.
They never found that buried hoard;
And yet their father was no fool.
Before he died he taught the golden rule:
     Work is the hidden reward.

REF. NO. 31)   AUTHOR(S)   **La Fontaine, translated by James Michie**

But things are falling neatly into place for my journal.
Phone's ringing as I take my seat and it turns out to be my
roommate's girlfriend Mara, calling right on the heels of
that 10:45 meeting. It's a sequence of events Mara and her
friends wouldn't dream of introducing without the word "jux-
taposition"--as it was Mara's get-together on Sunday that,
fanatically anti-corporate as it was, couldn't have been more
similar to the TQM session I just left.

"There you are, Mark Thornton." I'm supposed to be helping
Mara make her independent film. Well, video, but full-length.
She's caught me on the phone, at work, which is trouble.

"Here I am."

"There you are. What am I interrupting?"

"Well Mara, when you reach me at this number it means I'm
working...." then adding "for the Man" so I won't sound so
arch.

"Oh yes. Yeah, working for the Man is right. You worker
bee!"

"That's me. Ehm, what's on your mind?"

"What, is on, my mind...well we can start at Sunday?
Ah...could I suggest a word like 'intense?'"

"Intense."

"I mean could you even <u>handle</u> the <u>vibe</u> in that <u>room</u>? I
know, you put people like that in a room with each other and,
stand <u>back</u>, but I mean--fwooh!--didn't you feel like that
was, that it was..."

I feel like she's going to say "transcendent," or something biblical about mountains and islands shifting from
their resting places, but she just trails off. The languor
and whimsy in her voice mark (for an ear cauliflowered by 18
months in customer service) someone who could keep you on the
line for hours. She sounds like she's smoking, and I imagine
she's arranged across the divan in her bedroom, twisting the
phone cord around a finger or toe.

As Mara gropes for something important to say, the scene
from this past weekend starts reassembling itself. And only
the full-bore flashback is going to do here; there's a broader point I want to make about Mara's avant-garders and our
own practitioners of TQM, and the empty language in which

they've mired themselves....

Sunday: I'm being let into a fashionable downtown flophouse where Mara's con-
vened some 10 or 12 self-styled artists,
a mix of trust-fund bohemians like herself and some truly broke and desperate
people. The pretext is a movie that
Mara's supposed to have scripted and
blocked already, and today parts are
being assigned, rehearsals and screen
tests undertaken. Strewn about the room
is much expensive-looking audio, video
and lighting equipment, most of it being
hefted and fiddled with by a 'tech
staff' of dubious credentials.

So I'm greeted at her door by an
addled but not unattractive young woman
in Twiggy-style jumper and boots, who
leads me into the company of these
artists with the proclamation: "Mara,
the photographer's here." Well. I admit
to feeling a little pleased. Truth is
I'm here to act out any support roles
they might have written in, and to help
lug equipment and furnish sets, wherever
they need a pair of hands. But Mara's
also decided that with my 'photographer's eye' I might offer counsel on matters cinematographic.

It's about 11:00 in the morning but
the sunlight, filtering in through
nicotine-ambered glass curtains, takes

Fig. 1.14
Wrought iron
ashstand at
Mara's. The tray
is lime-tinted
depression
glass--kept
thinking it
couldn't accom-
modate another
butt and they
kept proving me
wrong.

on a quality of dusk. The mood here, what they might call
their 'milieu,' is best described as funereal, with conversation subdued to near formality and a heavy reliance on black
clothing. The air's heated and close, scented with incense and
clove cigarettes, over the undercurrent of tobacco smoke rising from Mara's 1970's rec-room furnishings, mostly from an
ancient shag rug that curls up an inch or two onto the base-
boards. For furniture there's a mini garage sale of seam-bust-
ed mattresses and boxsprings, one coverless futon mat crooked

into a corner, an assortment of stools, hassocks and patio
chairs and one giant thread-bare recliner. Mara's perched
in this last item, one hand lowering a campari and soda
from her mouth while the other fondles a string of mala-
chite rosary beads. She's consumed in conversation and
acknowledges my entrance with a wan smile. My roommate, her
boyfriend, is in the kitchen editing the script (turns out
he's trying to write one) and is not to be disturbed. Fine.
I introduce myself to a couple of people and am handed a
diary-sized notebook and a felt-tip pen with a mismatched
cap.

   It doesn't take long to identify the real 'visionary'
here, and it isn't Mara. She's more patroness and impre-
sario, I gather. The *chef artiste* is a guy named Meeshac,
who's sprawled face-up on a box spring next to a nattily
dressed woman, both of them looking as though they've fall-
en there from a great height. They're speaking quietly to
each other until Meeshac clears his throat and calls: "Um,
Mara?" Everyone falls silent, which is how I decide he's
the Mack Daddy.
   "Mm-hmmh?"
   "So. I'm--my character--he's searching for meaning obviously. But a kind of meaning for life and society, something universal like the state of the world, or like an
inner kind of spiritual or artistic truth?"
   "Both, I think. It's the same thing more or less, would-
n't you agree?"

Fig. I.15
Boot from Meeshac's
"Sherwood Forest"
collection

   "Sure, I buy that." Mara
visibly flattered. "It's," he
continues, "well, the back-
drop is the evil of the age,
you know, a society adrift,
disintegrating culture, like
literally dis-integrating,
like unravelling."
   "Corporations," offers a
rangy grad-student-looking
guy next to me. The woman who
led me in, slumped now on a

papasan, stifles a yawn, her palm flat against the "o" of
her mouth like a tired gesticulation of wonder.

"Yeah, all that. I could see his bosses just being like:
'blah-blah-blah,' not even having any lines just nonsense,
like the adults in Peanuts. So is this guy a total Goth?
No, he's got to be more archetypal, people have to be able
to...to access him. Let's say he starts off a 100% believ-
er, like rarin' to go and get a job, but he ends up utterly disillusioned, just sick of it all."

"You'll have to borrow some civilian clothes, for those
early scenes," says another young woman, winning a theatrical laugh from Meeshac. He sits up and wraps his legs
beneath him Indian-style. A great shock of frizzed hair is
swept off his forehead and bound with an Asian kind of
chopstick assemblage. His manner is that of a storyteller,
one whose story threatens to lapse in and out of song.

"We did the same kind of thing at the Black Box Stage.
Lucian helped out there too. Remember, Lucian? We didn't
even give it a title, barely even a script, just notes
scrawled on the insides of matchbooks really, so it was
different each time we did it, oh, like 3 or 4 times,
whatever. I was thinking we could do something like that
with this, like keep it loose. It'd be much more believ-
able like that. It would have resonance."

"I say we go total ad-lib," grad-student Lucian puts
in, "just set up a scene and shoot, leave it all to the
editing. That's the license of video, you know, we can
shoot as much as we want."

"Sure. We just get thousands of hours of improv, and
pare it down to like 90 minutes, just the really important footage. I see me surrounded by all these flannel
suits, I'm just like 'You're crucifying me!' Which, we
could have it be allegorical (I'm thinking out loud
again!), like the temptation of Christ, or his persecu-
tion, whichever. Have the scenes correspond to the stations of the cross, maybe. Completely religious over-
tones, but Western Orthodox, none of that kookie yang-
bang Oriental stuff. Although it's got to be toned,
the...pitch, has to be godless. Like maybe even apocalypse, post-holocaust Godot-type thing. Totally minimal-
ist. And like Nietzschean. Hugely emotional."

Don't speak unless
you can improve on
the silence.

Spanish proverb

55

"You guys have any idea when you want to have this thing finished?" I ask, thinking forward to thousands of hours of winging it with these people. Turns out to be precisely the wrong thing to say. They all smirk and look over to Meeshac.

"Oh what about budget, what about schedule," he says in a deep, mock-serious voice. "It's done when it's done, okay, that's my spiel for you on scheduling. This is going to be an organic kind of thing, I mean this is real stream-of-consciousness. Nothing...valid, ever gets handed down from a schedule or a budget, it has to grow up from the association of creatives with each other, it grows and feeds off of artistic interaction, and it is whatever it is. Does that, ah, help put you in touch with our project?" I affirm that it does.

It's now that I realize what I'm in for, and I want very badly to leave. There isn't going to be any movie at all. Just look at these action junkies. This is thrilling enough for them, bartering opinions with a sensation like Meeshac. This is plenty to have accomplished in a day. They just listen, rapt, as he explains how his last name has been lost to memory, leaving him ill-equipped to relate to this world of twice- and thrice-named individuals. He recounts much of the suffering he's undergone in service of art and things creative. He explains how a state of continual joblessness carries him above the herd of men who, like swine rooting after truffles, sully themselves with the matters of this world, pursuing objects whose value will ever be lost on them. I don't see why I couldn't have been warned about this.

I do end up with some interesting notes, of course:

•• Chandra, the woman with Meeshac, turns out to be a young Pakistani man named Michael. I will not hear him speak today. The only purpose he seems to serve is maintaining around Meeshac an air of exoticness and sexual ambiguity.

•• From Lucian's notebook, on the subject of non-linear thinking: "A pair of crossed lines will suggest for most the letter t or x, perhaps a crucifix or even a lug wrench; in the same datum, the artist might see an Edwardian gentleman, or

Godzilla advancing on Tokyo." Earnest discussion ensues.

•• I start keeping a tally of how many times the words creative, art and artistic are used. I keep it up for a half hour before I tire of that too. The cumulative total in this time is 22, thirteen attributable to Meeshac.

•• Travis has begun boring holes into the cover of a Cosmopolitan with an awl or an ice pick. He produces a bag of colored-metal jacks and glues one into each hole and laces them together with gold lamé thread. Meeshac suggests that he fix the covergirl with devil-horns and a Van Dyke, which he does with a laundry marker. He rises with his creation and leaves the room to photograph it, holding it carefully at eye-level as though it were some kind of wayfinding device or religious totem. Someone comments: "Nice one, Travis."

•• Go to check on my roommate in the kitchen. I find he hasn't written anything past the words 'Establishing shot:' on a legal pad. He's been in there getting high with a married Russian couple. He wants me to listen to their idea for an independent film, a modern interpretation of Crime and Punishment with Raskolnikov a young Russian immigrant in New York. Or a TV screenplay where your Joan Van Ark takes the role of Joan of Arc, hmm? How about Letter Man, the fellow in that children's show, goes raving and turns someone's dinner party into the Donner Party? Cartoon people set about eating one another? The three of them in fits by now. I tell them it makes more sense than the movie we're planning in the living room.

•• Sasha takes his notebook, and two others that have been abandoned on a coffee table, and starts juggling with them. Seeing this, Penny leaves the room and returns with three colored clubs, which he also begins to juggle. Simone attends to this with the video camera. It's the only time a camera will run all day.

Shortly after nightfall Mara suggests we adjourn to Blue Bodega, a coffee house three flights below her place, and the motion is heartily carried. I decline, pay my devoirs and take off. I close the door on Meeshac's explanation of why somebody's character, his own perhaps, ought to be blind, stricken thus, perhaps, in a moment of epiphany. Still no talk about where or when we might hold our next session.

So that was that, my foray with the artists. And my room-mate's going to answer for stranding me in there. People like that, when they organize in those numbers, you begin to call them a "troupe." Theater people, no doubt about it--or at least they once were--I can see them together in some high school production, staying in character even when they're backstage or walking between classes: "Hew-Heww, I'm keeping an eye on you, Artful Dodger!"; "Rest up, lads, for tomorrow we sail on the Pinafore!" Bothersome images, but Mara's living room was worse. In high school at least they might have accomplished something, even if it was only Man of LaMancha or whatever. At Mara's we had the time and equipment, and we had enough interested people, to begin creating something worthwhile. Instead, though, I sat and listened to them advance and react to an afternoon's worth of valueless decrees and opinions.

Actually producing anything would have involved compro-mise, you see, judgment, evaluation, all to the denigration of their art. As soon as you pander to someone else's idea of the creative product (a poem or photo or canvas or CD, in this case a video or even a script) you've begun to make merchandise of your art, so you haven't made art at all, have you? Progress smacks of linearity, production smacks of commercialism. The kind of logic that could drive you nuts.

If only for the setting, then, and the modes of dress and the vernacular, we might have had a TQM meeting. Business and anti-business, carried to ridiculous extremes, accom-plishing equal amounts of nothing. And the vernaculars aren't even that dissimilar. Different words, but in either case it's only words. Like a pre-written transcript for a period in which nothing definite will happen and from which nothing can arise. It's a shame too, because whether it was reinvigorating customer service or making an independent

film, I was all for it. But we got caught
in some dead-end system of communication,
or decorum, where the only "goal" is an
observation of rules. There was a great
deal of talk about "process," as in "I'm
not comfortable with that process" or "we
need to focus more on process before we can
scope the project out." But the process is,
you talk about process. That's it. Like
Mara sez, it's all an end in itself, this
creative exchange.

For adherents and practitioners the
rewards of the system are vast and self-
evident, emperor's-new-clothes style. It's
only when you step outside the living room,
or the conference room, that you begin to
nurture doubt. Pitcher asks if anyone can
explain the charter we've just written, and
his answer is silence. I spend seven hours
with the artists and what we get is some
murky theme of a generational archetype
searching for himself in the celibate winter of the late 1990's. So what. The thing
is, for Lon and Meeshac and anyone who lis-
tens to them, these are great advances. And
it makes sense to agree, to go along with
the program, if only to avoid ostracism or
having to apologize to your co-workers for
'indecorous conduct'....

So when Mara calls today, it's to proclaim
last Sunday an artistic triumph, and to see if
she can't make lightning strike twice in as
many weekends. She invites me back to the creative hotbed she's made of her living room,
only now we're to call it the "salon."

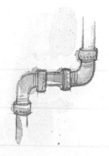

They pin much
imperial behavior
during the
decline of the
Roman Empire to
lead plumbing in
the palaces--won-
der if anyone's
checked ours.
It'd be nice to
have a reason
supplied for this
TQM behavior, or
at least for the
Caligula's-horse-
in-the-Senate
appointment of
Lon Baffert to
department head.
I could use the
affirmation, stop
wondering if it's
been me or them
this whole time.

59

Dada is a new tendency in art. One can tell this from the fact that until now nobody knew anything about it, and tomorrow everyone in Zurich will be talking about it....

How does one achieve eternal bliss? By saying dada. How does one become famous? By saying dada. With a noble gesture and delicate propriety. Till one goes crazy. Till one loses consciousness. How can one get rid of everything that smacks of journalism, worms, everything nice and right, blinkered, moralistic, europeanized, enervated? By saying dada. Dada is the world soul, dada is the pawnshop. Dada is the world's best lily-milk soap....

Each thing has its word, but the word has become a thing by itself. Why shouldn't I find it? Why can't a tree be called Pluplusch, and Pluplubasch when it has been raining? The word, the word, the word outside your domain, your stuffiness, this laughable impotence, your stupendous smugness, outside all the parrotry of your self-evident limitedness. The word, gentlemen, is a public concern of the first importance.

| REF. NO. 32) | *See notes, pp. 148-151* | AUTHOR(S) | **Hugo Ball** |

Here's an excerpt from "The First Dada Manifesto" of 1916, and the latest from "The Human Dynamics Program for Individual and Team Empowerment" — yes, really.

Program Content:

The understanding of the different needs and characteristics of the various personality dynamics is used throughout the program in addressing those aspects of personal development most crucial to optimizing both individual and team performance, and to the exercise of effective leadership. The various aspects of the program are organized in modular form each building on the other in a natural progression. The progression of the program is shown in figure 1....

1. Who am I?
2. Who are you?
3. What are our distinct communication needs?
4. What are the different languages we speak?
5. What is the function of each communicator?
6. What is the direction of empowerment for each personality dynamic?
7. What are the different processes of the personality dynamics in task solution?
8. How do we function best together in teams?
9. How do we bridge the gaps?
10. What exercises can we practice to promote and sustain our growth?

. . . .

It is, indeed, extremely difficult to glimpse a meaning anywhere. And the search for it is hopelessly complicated by the fact that there are far too many "meanings" already—millions of short-lived, short-sighted, short-winded ad hoc meanings which seem uncommonly sensible to all who are struck with them, the more so the more senseless they are.

Carl G. Jung

II

. . . .

Intermezzo:

Lunch at
Mr. Hsu's

At 11:30, Monday through Friday, Mr. Hsu throws open the doors to his eponymous downtown eatery. The scene is rather like the children's first scramble through Willy Wonka's factory. A flood of patrons race along booths that crowd the left- and right-hand walls, there to have orders quickly filled before a musical-chairs dash to the banquet tables. The atmosphere is strictly no-nonsense, a place where food is unromantically dispensed and consumed, where the term 'eatery' is convincingly applied. From their ramshackle kitchenfronts, vendors produce, with the flair of so many assembly-line workers, specialties of Mandarin, Cantonese, Szechuan, Polynesian, Thai, Japanese and Korean cooking, from the authentic to the wholly Americanized. Between the north-facing staff and their south-facing counterparts is a series of long slatted tabletops raised on concrete blocks, each table flanked by a pair of equally long picnic-style benches. The far wall in the eatery is notable only for a waist-high door of quilted metal, through which bussers are continually stooping for reasons obscure. There is, above the bustle, an air of temporariness here, like you'd feel in a carnival midway; it's as though Mr. Hsu, after 15 years in the city, is still trying to decide whether or not he'll make a go at the eatery business.

From noon to 2:30 you find a great cross-section of the city assembled here in a boisterous motley. Eating cheek-and-jowl, passing along shared condiments and likely engaged in discussion are suits and tradesmen, tourists and Chinatown locals, cops and transients. No point in coming with a group, since seats are available singly or not at all. That's actually part of the charm for me, the roulette-style seating, the forced bonhomie of a revolving cast of strangers....

I start making my way over to Mr. Hsu's Chinatown Eatery as soon as Mara lets me off the phone. Outside it's one of those sharp-focus summer days that already hints of fall. A real peach, not even these city road crew guys with their backhoes and steamrollers and jackhammers can put a dent in it. Noon has posted a perfect white disc of sun overhead, the sunlight passing through a row of citified maples and spangling the sidewalk beneath with a filigree as bright and neat as scissored paper; a dispiriting city sidewalk transformed, annoyingly, into some happy country lane. The sky's marbled with just a few fair-weather cirrus clouds, and coming out from the trees I cock my head to look up at it sidelong, not in appreciation but like I might start shaking a fist at it, make people think I'm some lunatic castigating his gods. Seems terribly unfair that I'd have been boxed off in a climate-controlled office today. I have to fight the urge to just keep walking, I mean like walking straight out of the city.

I am alarmed when it happens that I have walked a mile into the woods bodily, without getting there in spirit. In my afternoon walk I would fain forget all my morning occupations and my obligations to society. But it sometimes happens that I cannot easily shake off the village. The thought of some work will run in my head and I am not where my body is—I am out of my senses. In my walks I would fain return to my senses.

REF. NO. 33) *See notes, pp. 148-151*   AUTHOR(S)   **Henry David Thoreau**

Slogging along like this, fists in pockets, when I pass Spoons. He's slouched in the shade of a huge granite plinth outside the post office, in that discarded posture of his. "How about some change, Mark?" he wants to know.

"I'm busted."

"The hell you're busted, I hear it in your pockets."

"That's just my keys."

"Just your keys."

"Yeah but catch me after lunch."

"A'ight, if I'm still here."

Today Mr. Hsu has lost his lunch crowd to the weather, which--well I'd best stop thinking about the weather. But the Eatery's whole mess-hall fraternity dynamic falls flat when the place isn't jammed. Suits me. I cart my lunch over to an empty corner of the room--or nearly empty. I'm not even seated when I catch sight of John McKenna from behind, a couple rows up and bent over a stone pot of rice noodles. John's a formatter in our design group, and I've been meaning to corner someone from design, ask some career-type questions. He used to work straight production until a month or so ago, and I met him a while before that, so I can resituate myself opposite him without too much formality.

"Hey-hey, I don't think I've seen you at Mr. Hsu's before, Mark," he sez as I pluck a couple clean-looking chopsticks from a lazy susan.

"No? I feel like I'm some kind of fixture here. So's half the company, I think, but you can sit two seats over from someone here and never know. Relatives, celebrities, heads of

Fig. II.1: Signage, Mr. Hsu's Chinatown Eatery

Chopsticks, successively lit, appear to fall into bowl of rice

63

Figure II.2: Golfbear

There's a guy at Mr. Hsu's with his back to me, whose t-shirt is worth mentioning. "Golfbear" it says across the top, and again at the bottom: "Golfbear." And in between there are indeed a little bunch of bear golfers, caddies and spectators, all disporting themselves about an incompetently imagined fairway. I wouldn't think the golfbears are playing too expert a round, or that the others could be troubled to notice, as none of the golfbears have any eyes. Scattered over the t-shirt, by way of explanation, is the nonsense phrase "Fun of Golf" in a variety of fonts and sizes.

state. You'd never know. I saw Burt Ward get take-out right over there, nobody bothered him." Which is true, but I need to take a breath now before I get worked up.

Groping inexpertly with my chopsticks, then, while John tilts his bowl up and goes poking in it, kind of sullenly, sez 'fuck it' and brings it right to his mouth. Gentility isn't expected at Mr. Hsu's, just the courtesy of not observing your tablemates in the act of eating.

Have to get right to business here because he looks to be finishing up: "So, mind if I ask how you're liking it, up there in design?" Pffft! his soup goes spurting across the table—actually it doesn't, John lowers the bowl, steadily, from his lip.

"Mmm," he considers. "Up there in design..." That voice of John's is so deep, it's felt as much as heard (I imagine he'd have been hounded by glee clubs in college). And when he needs it to connote gravity, like now, it dips even lower. "What can I say. It was the right move, for me. Unquestionably, I'd been running resin-coated paper for three years down there. Absolutely bored as hell, you know." Dogs in the streets and alleys of Chinatown suddenly angling their heads toward Mr. Hsu's. "It wasn't even a career move, like a resume move, in spite of what you'd think. More like, well you've seen the room with the processor. 11 to 7 in that hot-box? Forget about it."

"I wouldn't last a shift in there, or scanning either."

"Yeah but in scanning, there you've got other people to talk to, and some of the retouch work they do's pretty involved. The RC-paper man works alone, remember that. They sent me a bunch of derelicts to train as assistants or replacements, one every month or so when I complained, just throwing me bones. I think I must have trained a dozen college kids and not a one worked out. Senior Management's like 'You're too good to replace.' Yeah. I was the only guy who'd stand for that job, they ought to have said. Until I was like enough, you people. The raises they offered me were probably 'hefty' by their standards but, you know, it wasn't about money at that point."

I could have expected this, that he'd be more inclined to talk about the horrors of his old position than the glamour of the new one, such as it is. Two reasons why: first he's being careful to avoid condescension. John's done his time downstairs and knows well the tenderness of ego down there, the quickness to take offense. He's not going to say: 'in design I finally get to use my brain,' because for anyone outside design that takes on the force of insult.

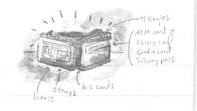

Left my wallet on the table at Mr. Hsu's some Friday in February. Came back on Sat. to find it right where I'd left it, not one item missing.

The second reason is, he knows how little separates us, and he's not so firmly ensconced up there that an aspiring designer wouldn't make him uneasy. John's like a newlywed anxious to keep his wife from the company of bachelors. Most designers, in my experience, are like that to a degree, they try to 'help' you off that career path. They love to tell you there are more kids in design school than designers currently working. Even well-heeled agency people tell you not to bother applying until you've graduated from the right programs at the right colleges and then interned at the right places, and actually, don't bother even then.

John isn't that hung up, but neither can he be fully encouraging: "I should say that this was the right thing for me, for my individual case. I don't know if it would work out for everyone. Why uhh, why did you want to ask?"

"Well I didn't want to put you on the spot here—"

"—No, no not at all—"

"—but, and I'm not considering a move to design, that's not why I'm asking. It's just, it's not happening in CS for me."

"Yeah, what's it like there?"

"Honestly? I feel like I'm being punished for something. I don't know for what." Beginning to sound rehearsed, here.

"Sucks, I know that feeling, I know that." He's gathering his things, shuffling in a half-crouch along the bench toward a wastebasket. "You ought to talk to Rebby if you can get some of her time. She could definitely tell you where to start."

"Yeah I ought to just call her. I've heard that. I'm trying, I don't know, I'm hoping to do something with...I don't know, photography?" There. Finally. "I mean I know every pinhead who can point a camera gets that idea sooner or later. I guess I'd ask her some things about, you know, that end of the business."

John's markedly relieved. I'm not angling for a position like his after all. Should have said that up front. "Hoo, photography. You should know, Mark, everyone's going to tell you to forget it, it's one of the toughest job markets to break into. So what, though? Plenty of people are making a living at it, and there's turnover there like anywhere else. They say, find what you're good at, what you like to do, and it all gets sorted out. The money doesn't come for a while, but again you know, so what?"

"That's right, well, thanks. I'm not even sure about photography, maybe something to do with that, though, who knows. But eh, sorry to turn your lunch into career corner, here."

"Not a problem, not a problem. I'll bring it up with Rebby. I can't tell you a whole hell of a lot, but she's someone who can."

1:25 PM -- Spoons: Freedom's Just Another Word...

On the way back I find Spoons, predictably, outside the post office where I left him. And where his wedge of shade has grown by almost a yard with the sun's procession. He spends his nights wandering Chinatown but he'll be found right here during the day, weather permitting, playing a French horn. Though I think 'playing' is a misleading term for what he does, 'experimenting' is more like it, in a way he might experiment with an object he's only come across minutes ago. He disassembles it and oils it, reassembles it and puts his mouth to the mouthpiece and rails at passersby through the bell, not musically but like literally yelling at them. Occasionally he manages a scale but mostly he leaves it on a blanket at his side and flips his bottom lip out at the calves and knees of the city's working class.

Fig. II.3
Spoons' case

That's what he's up to now, with a sign propped in his instrument case: No Money, No Music. It's an arrangement everyone seems comfortable with. Nor does he seem to notice when I drop him some change. "Thank you," he says after a spell. "Now back to work." He leaves the French horn undisturbed beside him, so I guess he means for me to get back to work.

The plight of the homeless is not a subject I'm prepared to treat, but I will say this about Spoons. I can't imagine what preoccupies or motivates a guy like this, what sort of demons he's freighted with or what aspirations he holds, but I can guess what his principal concern is. He's bored, he's just as bored as me.

III

· · · · · · ·

Snappin' the
Crackers

1:35 PM -- "Colas" with Lon

*F*ind myself playing a shell game on the Internet in which I'm
faced with three walnut shells, two concealing head shots of
George Peppard and the third one of Mr. T, the object being of
course to flush out T, who breaks cover with some peppery words of
congratulation. *Ain't nothin' but luck fool, come at me again.* Lon
rears up behind me with no more warning than that fennel-scent of his,
which is almost like the smell of black licorice. I hide the browser
but, I think, not quite quickly enough. He grips the backrest on my
chair and gives it a vigorous shake even as I'm turning to face him.
Then he asks me a strange thing: "Been to lunch yet, Thornton?"

I blink. "Uh yeah, Lon, I got back like ten minutes ago. I thought
you watched me take my name off the board."

"Fair enough. I'm taking <u>my</u> lunch now, finally. C'mon out with me,
will you? I'll grab you a cola." A 'cola'?

"Sure, but I just got back, there's a ton--" Lon's face goes slack
and out comes a gun he's made of his thumb and forefinger: "It's an
offer you can't refuse," he sez, and metes out a laugh at this bit of
cleverness.

Managers are much more fearful of the future than they have ever been before.... At the most basic level, they are terrified of losing their jobs. First in the United States, then in Britain, and now in Europe and Japan, companies have broken with the convention that a job in management is a job for life.

Even if they have survived the latest round of restructuring, managers still have to come to terms with radically redesigned jobs. What, after all, are they actually supposed to do when they "manage"? Are they strategy setters? Sergeant majors in business suits? Coaches? Amateur psychotherapists? In the old days of steep hierarchies and deferential workers, such heretical questions never arose: senior managers set strategy, subdivided tasks into their component parts, and designed incentive schemes, and their juniors supervised workers and bawled them out if they slacked off. But now that computers are putting information in the hands of more and more employees and decision making is being devolved to front-line workers, the traditional sources of managerial authority are disappearing....

Allan Katcher, an American psychologist, has asked senior American executives what they would least want their subordinates to know about them. In 19 out of the 20 cases the answer was the same. They feared that their subordinates would learn how inadequate they felt in their jobs.

REF. NO. 34) AUTHOR(S) **John Micklethwait and Adrian Wooldridge**

This insecurity leaves some managers — like Lon, it seems — not only open to, but desperate for, any management fad promising results: you undergo

this training and perform these exercises and you will become an effective manager. This is how your Jay Gatherses stay in business. (More of Micklethwait and Wooldridge's argument on p. 74.)

So there I am, leaving the office to go and get 'colas' with Lon. Our elevator ride and stroll through the lobby are predictably stiff and subdued, neither of us meeting the others' eyes. We're talking about, I don't know, the All-Star break, the pennant race, Lon waiting for the proper setting to have this out, whatever it is, and me thinking back to all the heads we turned in leaving the office together. We jog across an inter- section and up to the Publick House, whose heavy medieval-looking door Lon holds open for me. I imagine they would sell 'colas' here, but this is an Irish ale house. So I'm wondering if this is what happens when you get fired. Or promoted.

Fig. III.1
They've named the patisserie downstairs "La Vie est un Croissant," life is a croissant. And don't I know it.

We take up stools at the bar. Here Lon unfastens his wristwatch and sets it in front of us, the face tilted up on the clasp so we can read the time. He taps the crystal and nods at it, and I nod at it too and say "Yep" for no reason at all. The proprietor sidles up with a sanguine greeting for me because we're well acquainted, though he's got the good sense not to call me by name in front of Lon.

"How about a look at your lunch menu," sez Lon, "and he's going to...ehm, what'll you have, there, Thornton?" Now if Lon wanted to have a Coke with me we could have stopped at the patisserie in the lobby. We're seated at a bar. They have to serve food here because it's the law, but the Publick House is not known as a lunch spot. I order a draft, damn it all.

The bartender has his fists bunched up against the inside lip of the bar, except for one rigid index finger that he's playing from Lon to me and back, like a little metronome. "Drink for you?" he asks Lon.

Fig. III.2
Publick House front door

"Nn...nyaah'll have a club soda, no lime," is how my manager responds. Well. The finger's back on me again, the bar- man's eyebrows arched high on his fore- head. But I let the order stand. I believe that Lon wants to take me out for a beer. And so long as at least one of us orders a beer, we can be properly said to

Intro V/O: He may be calling the shots from 9 to 5, but at home it's every man for himself! Get ready to move in with the Bafferts, where it ain't Father Knows Best!

Baffert living room: furniture is strictly 1975 Sears Showroom. Avocado, turquoise, harvest gold. Starburst clock, machine-grained wainscotting. Two kids in sailor suits contend in foreground over an all-day sucker, a second lollipop having fallen and lodged in the carpet.

SFX: Urban clamor—traffic, jackhammers, car-alarms, shouting neighbors, &c.

Baffert enters door at stage center to applause. Staggers, blocking ears, stage left to an open window, closes it and secures latch. Sighs.

SFX: Breaking glass

Bottle sails through window-pane stage right

SFX: noise from street, louder than before

Baffert: (shaking fist at window) Punks!

Sylvia from offstage: Shaddup, Lon! You're upsetting the children. (scattered laughter)

Baffert: Ooh, sorry Peanuts.

(cont'd on p. 71)

have "gone out for a beer." As in, "I had to come down on Thornton this morning, but I gave him time to cool off and then took him out for a beer." So a beer arrives for me and I just look at it there on the bar.

But just the advent of booze seems to have done the trick for Lon, who settles into his seat and for the love of God stops drumming his cordovans on the foot rail. I take a modest tug on my drink, which will count as humoring him.

"So," he sez at length. "Whaddya think I ought to do with Jason Pitcher?" and I swear he's picked up some kind of slur. I've seen guys do this, start acting giddy in bars whether or not they're being served.

"Pitcher? Don't know. Get him into therapy."

"No, no, come on Thornton. I like Jason"—unconvincing here—"and I know you do too. It's, the thing is, as a manager I have to watch out for guys like him. Pitcher's smart, he's a great addition to the team, but a manager has to keep an eye on morale. I have to anticipate. And I know how things can break down, I have to see it a few steps ahead, like playing checkers. You were there for that meeting today. Which, by the way I lost my cool. I said some things"—he raises a palm to me, warding off an interruption I hadn't considered—"no, I did, I went overboard. I said some things that were very unprofessional. I'll have to recant much of that, you'll get an e-mail today. That was just out of line."

"Lon, no, that, I think"—and so forth, as I ought.

"Thanks but no, there's no excuse for an outburst like that. A—and we had a confrontation this morning, you and I did, and that's not sitting well with me either." Lon being genuine, I believe. Even if it's just the booze working on me that's working on him. "I have to. And this is difficult to explain. As a manager, I'm responsible for your performance, you Mark Thornton and you the CS team, in general. And I really am on your team--I know, but appearances aside. It's my ass on the line with Senior Management, right next to yours. I'm there to run interference for you guys: things like your coming in late? Think about that, Senior Management never hears about that until it's a serious issue, like when it might cost you your job. The thing is, if it reaches that point, well I'm not supposed to let it, so I haven't been doing my job, you see?"

I nod sagely. "Lon, this morning was totally justified, I mean, I was the one who was late. I was the embarrassed one, I was late again. Which I'm going to try and not let happen. I have no problem with how that was handled, believe me. My problem's with me."

"Well good, thanks." Now we can move on, perhaps to the real reason why we've gone out for beers. "Now I watch you closely, Thornton, I tell you this in confidence. I watch you even more closely than the others and I'll tell you why. And it's not a bad thing even though it seems that way when we have our run-ins. I know, I can see you're an ambitious kid, excuse me, young man. In the way I was at your age." As Lon continues, and as I continue to drain my pint, his John Wayne drawl becomes more pronounced and his gestures more abrupt and histrionic. I swear this is true. "Take this TQM journal you're doing today. I think that idea's fantastic. And I can tell you something, Senior Management really applauds this kind of thing...." Lon suddenly cagey: "...Which, by the way, you've written up our little incident today, presumably, and the meeting we had, my outburst and that

Kids: (stop fighting long enough to thrust out tongues at Baffert)

Baffert: (addressing camera again, shrugs) Won't I ever catch a break? (raucous applause; this is clearly his signature line)

Kids: (in chorus) Da-ad, are we going to the Truck Pull this weekend?

Baffert: Damn it all, we've already been to the Truck Pull, I told you this weekend we'd--

Kids: (in chorus) Mo-om?

Sylvia offstage: Yes of course we can go.

Baffert: (double-take) But I--! But you--! That does it, Sylvia. I'm leaving this house. Ehh, for good!

Sylvia offstage: Where do you think you're going Lon? You just got home.

Baffert: I thought I'd jump off the balcony, if you want to know the truth.

Sylvia offstage: Well if you're going out come back with a carton of smokes. Or don't come back.

Kids: (evil laughter)

Baffert: (addresses camera, shrugs) Won't I ever catch a break? (laughter and applause; fadeout)

business...?"

"Well, but only in a summary kind of way. I'm just record-
ing events. I'm not supposed to editorialize so much. And
Senior Management never sees any of this, it's confidential.
They only read the summary brief I have to prepare when it's
over."

Lon stretches his back and pinions his shoulders to con-
ceal what has to be relief, and carries on with elaborate
nonchalance: "Well alright, but I'll tell you this anyway.
Not that, I mean you write whatever you want in your journal,
I just want to let you in on some things. You're an ambitious
young man, like me, like I said. That's what put me in that
office, got me that title of manager, I mean I know I wasn't
picked out in any popularity contest. I have no illusions
about that." Looking balefully into his club soda. "I'll tell
you this, though. Nobody wants the middle manager's job. I'll
bet that's a strange thing to hear coming from me, what with
my office and all, and you guys plugging away out there in
your cubicles...."

I tell him about Pitcher and 'Two Men With Cudgels.' Which
should help Pitcher's cause somewhat.

"He said that? Yeah, no flies on Jason. It's a thankless
job. I don't ask for sympathy, I mean it's my own drive that
landed me here, same thing as'll spring me out--not that I'm
anxious to leave, you understand. But a couple more years and
that's that. Stay too long at a spot like this, any one
place, and you stagnate, the job you love begins to devour
you." Looking at the tiers of liquor bottles before us now,
addressing them as he might some vast audience. "So I put in
a couple more, three years. But yeah it's not an easy job.
You know what a trial Senior Management can be"--he checks
himself, focusing back on me--"err, they have a job to do and
they do it well, we all know that, I mean the company's going
gangbusters. But their job involves bearing down on me to
make things run right. And then I've got you people pushing
the opposite way." His forehead falls to the web of his thumb
and forefinger but then, just as suddenly, it's back up where
it ought to be. "Don't take this wrong, but look at the hand
I've been dealt in terms of a staff. You people are a damn
difficult bunch. Damn difficult."

I own up to this and he turns, satisfied, back to the bottles. "I'm like the manager of a bunk baseball team, you know, and who do the owners screw over when they don't win, or when fans stop showing up for games? No matter what the reason, the weather, tough schedule, injuries? They go right after the manager. Most nervous guy in the game, is the manager. I try, you know, I'm in there every day trying to keep you guys on track."

He's right, I consider. He's been saddled with a bunch of overeducated, oversensitive young adults languishing in a kind of career layover, underutilized and bored. And the punchline for Lon is that Senior Management bases their evaluation of him on our performance. He knows how weighty an adversary he's got in our apathy, and he knows his fear-and-money management style won't eliminate it, only put it off in some dark recess where it'll anneal into something permanent and truly sinister. He can only hope he'll be gone by then, or that we will.

And now there's the added pressure of TQM, the latest Machiavellian belief system to find a mouthpiece in Lon. He's got to ram this program through at a time when morale in general, and our fondness for him in particular, have reached historically low ebbs. And if he can't, well, Senior Management will find someone who can.

Lon's managed to order a Black Forest and it comes up, conveniently, just as he's searching for some kind of closer. He settles for "I dunno, Thornton. I hope some of that made sense to you."

I tell him it surely does, that I appreciate the bind he's in, that I'll do what I can to help work things through, that I'll be leaving so he can eat that awful-looking sandwich without an audience. He gestures to the last quarter of my beer.

"You going to finish that one, hombre? Your cerveza?"

"Nah, you're welcome to it, Lon. I'm gonna go tell some Senior Manager you're tying one on at the Publick House."

"—"

"That's...I'm kidding about that, I'd never say that." Lon with his head thrown back now, braying like I've brought off some tremendous coup of a joke.

> Anxiety is that range of distress which attends willing what cannot be willed.
>
> Leslie H. Farber

73

Yet many people who end up in such managerial positions are promoted not for their managerial skills but for their excellence in other jobs—as engineers or lawyers or editorial writers. In their former jobs, they no doubt despised management theory. Perhaps, they despise it still; but now that they are going to be evaluated on the basis of their managerial abilities, they reluctantly fall under its spell. So they turn to the people who "know," guiltily buying a book on management, then organizing a conference, with, say, a consultant from McKinsey to act as a "facilitator."

To these anxiety-ridden men and women, management books offer a rare source of security. The most obvious beneficiaries are those fringe thinkers who concentrate on the individual rather than the organization: hence the charm of Stephen Covey's new-age psychotherapy (*The Seven Habits of Highly Effective People*, 1989) and of motivational gurus such as Anthony Robbins. However, managerial angst has also helped brass tacks authors who provide their readers with a more general explanation of what exactly is happening to them. For instance, Charles Handy's *The Age of Unreason* (1989) addresses the disappearance of jobs for life. A follow-up, *The Empty Raincoat* (1995), looks at the widespread feeling that life is out of balance, with some people working round the clock and others having nothing to do. Even fairly straightforward management books often come in packages designed to appeal to the nervous.... The ideal "unique selling proposition" for a management book is something along the lines of "Buy me or else you will not be among the elite who will avoid being downsized out of a job or put on a short-term contract."

REF. NO. 35   AUTHOR(S) **John Micklethwait and Adrian Wooldridge**

The Seven Habits are habits of *effectiveness*. Because they are based on principles, they bring the maximum long-term beneficial results possible. They become the basis of a person's character, creating an empowering center of correct maps from which an individual can effectively solve problems, maximize opportunities, and continually learn and integrate other principles in an upward spiral of growth.... First, your growth will be *evolutionary*, but the net effect will be *revolutionary*.... You will come to know yourself in a deeper, more meaningful way—your nature, your deepest values and your unique contribution capacity. As you live your values, your sense of identity, integrity, control, and inner-directedness will infuse you with both exhilaration and peace.

REF. NO. 36   *See notes, pp. 148-151*   AUTHOR(S) **Stephen Covey**

- Today I will commit myself to detachment. I will allow myself and those around me the freedom to be as they are. I will not rigidly impose my idea of how things should be. I will not force solutions on problems, thereby creating new problems. I will participate in everything with detached involvement.
- Today I will factor in uncertainty as an essential ingredient of my experience. In my willingness to accept uncertainty, solutions will spontaneously emerge out of the problem, out of the confusion, disorder, and chaos.

REF. NO. 37   *See notes, pp. 148-151*   AUTHOR(S) **Deepak Chopra**

The smell of wet dog augurs a visit from Traci "Flying Nun" Vendler, Human Resources princess and Senior Management adjunct. The Flying Nun reference is from this preposterous rainhat she sports as often in fair weather as foul. She owns three chocolate labs too, and I don't know if she's rolling around in their kennel with them but the air around her brings that image to mind. Evidence of this, too, is found on her clothes, which have taken on the look of those hair-shirts worn by medieval penitents, except her guilt's so acute it's earned her a whole doghair outfit.

Anyhow, what's drawn Traci into her orbit around CS is tonight's TQM love-in with Jay Gathers. And you'd think Senior Management were taking us to the circus, to hear her bill the event. Jay's seminars aren't like lectures at all, you see, but like shows--*extravaganzas*--and you have no idea what an inspiration one man can be until you see him, he's going to surprise, invigorate, just flat-out amaze us, I mean there's a reason he gets all that money to speak--but I should say per-form, shouldn't I...?

That Traci can talk wallpaper right off the walls, because-- and it's why, I suppose--she's the HR manager. Positive, garru-lous, sunny, well-liked. This is the slot in the company, in life, for which she's been ordained, and her being there allows us to believe in things like right livelihood; her example reminds us that not all people land where they are by default or coincidence or duress, and not everyone's just doing time between weekends--in some jobs, for some people, there's a deep sense of *belonging* or *correctness*. Which begins to sound like metaphysics, but how else to describe Traci in HR?

I'm even going to say there are com-panies where this is the norm, this shared metaphysical sense of destination. And though the idea takes on properties of myth by the time it reaches a depart-ment like mine, I've heard it enough, from old co-workers who've gone on to their professional places in the sun, to buy it. There are young adults in this

Fig. III.3:
Traci's hat

Want to be a: rock star;
writer of fiction; feckless
heir/heiress; ranch hand;
Club Med steward; commercial
artist (art director, photog'er); sex industry king-
pin; actor; fine artist
(photog, sculptor, painter);
monk/hermit; want to "work
with kids"; stuntman

Can't because: Lack talent;
market's too tight/everyone
wants to be one; would
starve/doesn't pay; would
eventually get bored with
it; insecure future; would
have to move to NY/LA; would
have nothing left to com-
plain about; travails of
Evel Knievel instruct
against it

Continue to entertain the
idea because: am
improving/taking a course;
"I must create"; overabundance of convention in life;
related to notion of self-
worth or individuality; have
a friend/relation clearing
room in the field; "just
talking about it keeps me
going"; hope-inspiring example of Kaptain Robbie Knievel

very city going to work in their
weekend clothes, who are doing at
work what they'd as soon be doing
at home for free, who are meeting
their professional peers outside the
office because they actually like
to associate, and lingering at work
because that's where they feel most
comfortable. Really.

An idiot-savant named Glenn Tilday
worked in imagesetting here for three
months, he's one example. They fired
him because instead of running film
he just sat there animating his own
3-D models of traincars—but now
someone else is paying him like a
mandarin to render video game
scenery from home. Another guy from
shipping, with no less a name than
'Pere Upanishade,' was writing CGI
scripts for his band's website until
his roommates convinced him to sell
a few. Now he's authoring share-ware
for some startup developer.

I suppose I'm happy—I try to
be—for Glenn and Pere and the handful of other departees sending word
back from Babylon. I think they
think we like to hear from them too.
They all seem to have landed in one
high-tech startup or another, where
everyone's under 30 like in Logan's
Run. It isn't as though high-tech is
cornering the morale market, and
plenty of these startups end in
fistfights, I know. But all we hear
about is the thrill of breaking
ground in the technology market, the
motivational rewards of sharehold-
ing, the dominion of ideas and the
death of authority. We hear about
training and brainstorming sessions

and feedback loops that sound like legitimate versions of our TQM. And climates of morale ranging from Outward Bound gang-trauma to what psychologists describe as a "florid" state of psychosis—this, of course, reckoned a good thing.

I'd like to say I rejoice in their successes, but I really don't, now that I think of it. Back here in CS, my day lengthens with every happy postcard or e-mail. Every day that brings stasis and procrastination for me seems to bring change and movement and attainment to someone else. People are finding their rightful place in the working world and I'm here in CS like Disney's in Europe. With no better idea of where I belong than, simply, not here.

Is this true, though? You seem to have _some_ idea of where you might be more content: refer to p.32, or your conversation with John McKenna. Be careful not to let your frustrations devolve into despair.

If you choose to represent the various parts in life by holes upon a table, of different shapes— some circular, some triangular, some square, some oblong—and the persons acting these parts by bits of wood of similar shapes, we shall generally find that the triangular person has got into the square hole, the oblong into the triangular, and a square person has squeezed himself into the round hole. The officer and the office, the doer and the thing done, seldom fit so exactly that we can say they were almost made for each other.

REF. NO. 38) *See notes, pp. 148-151* AUTHOR(S) **Sydney Smith, 1850**

. . . .

People, especially the young, think that they want all the freedom they can get, but it is very demanding, very difficult to think through who you are and what you do best.... To build achieving organizations, you must replace power with responsibility.... The new organizations need to go beyond senior/junior polarities to a blend with sponsor and mentor relations. In the traditional organization— the organization of the last 100 years—the skeleton, or internal structure, was a combination of rank and power. In the emerging organization, it has to be mutual understanding and responsibility.

REF. NO. 39) *See notes, pp. 148-151* AUTHOR(S) **Peter F. Drucker**

2:10 PM -- A Conversational Template for the Mercenary Professional (or, In Defense of a Meaningless Job)

But who keeps us up to date with Glenn and Pere? Why, Glenn and Pere do. Who are as free as anyone to misrepresent the facts. A caveat here is, beware of anyone 'relishing' a job that a human being couldn't possibly enjoy. And even if the facts check out, there's still a difference between forced assimilation or learned acceptance and true professional fulfillment, between an impressive job and a calling. But I actually hear a great deal of that, people who start in describing their job and end up making a case for it. That's the alternative to all this search, is to stay put and work on your soft shoe. With enough practice you'll convince everyone that you're just where you want to be. The rule for listeners is, the longer the job description, the more bombastic. Here, for instance, is the script that about half my college classmates were reading off of at our last reunion:

Note: statements of time elapsed will recur throughout, becoming increasingly impassioned and decreasingly complex, until a simple exclamation (10 years!) is used to punctuate each conversational turn, accompanied by a firm thigh-swatting, a raised glass, or the seizure of one's temples or lower back.

A preamble deals with expressions of wonder at the passage of time, a review of the more extraordinary changes undergone by classmates, a listing of reunion events and the likelihood of your attendance thereto. Conversation will either founder here or move directly to career-forum, for which this script can be followed to the word.

(Tug on beer or punch) Um yeah. I've joined on at (firm), actually now they're calling me a (job title, sarcastically inflected). Whatever that means. It's crazy. If anyone told me back at (sorority/fraternity/campus bar) that I'd be (single-phrase job description using active verb), I'd have been: 'Oh I'm sorry, no, there's been a mistake, I'm the one who's going to work with kids, travel, gonna live somewhere where they don't use money. You can keep your Wall Street American Dream, man, just leave me Rimbaud and Toni Morrison and calculus and all that.' What the hell do you know at 21? (examine beer or punch, swirl thoughtfully) Got to do it, got to do it. And I'll tell you this: things have really worked out. Can't say it's easy, but you won't hear me complain about the hours. Heard (classmate) talking about 100-hour weeks, doing what? (job description, nearly identical to your own, huge ironic drawl) None of that for me, thanks. Meanwhile I get to see how the market works, from the inside, it's

fascinating. And I'm in there watching it happen, making it happen, in my
own little way, heh, sometimes not so little. Anyhow, it took a while but
I'm completely hooked, I need that rush. I take vacations when I want, any
time, I was ten days in (fashionably rugged coastal escape), but by the end
I'm going bananas, bored as hell. Where's my fax? Who do we lunch today? I'm
climbing the walls. Things change when they've got you using your brain,
I'll tell you. It's weird, I'd say my job is 90% problem-solving, I mean in
that way they draw heavily on your creativity. I know that isn't a word people associate with the field, but what else would you call it? They can get
any blockhead to (do something rudimentary you spend a great deal of time
doing); that's nowhere. It's all intellectual capital now. But, whatever.
Anyway, the ('chicks' if man, 'boys' if woman) in this company: this is a
real starting lineup. The distraction's getting chronic. We're a pretty young
company, actually, I mean the (your home city) branch. Our district manager,
totally cool, I'd guess no older than 35. After last quarter, our numbers
are in and, I mean, (s/he) knows we're busting our asses, (s/he) rents out
the (unlikely site for office party: aquarium, chem lab, Civil War bunker),
leaves us with an open bar and is like: see you on Monday! Things like that.
And I'll tell you something, the money does not suck. (If it's your 10th
reunion or later, you'll want to name salary figure with confidential air,
inflate 10%, add "Oh and bonuses, stock options and that? Hoah, daddy. I
mean, there's got to be a point where you stop counting....")

A man wants to earn money in order to be happy, and his whole effort and the best of a life are
devoted to the earning of that money. Happiness is forgotten; the means are taken for the end.... The
most destitute men often end up by accepting illusion. That approval prompted by the need for
peace inwardly parallels the existential consent. There are thus gods of light and idols of mud. But it
is essential to find the middle path leading to the faces of man.

| REF. NO. 40 | See notes, pp. 148-151 | AUTHOR(S) | **Albert Camus** |

. . . .

In its widest possible sense, however, *a man's Self is the sum total of all that he* CAN *call his*, not
only his body and his psychic powers, but his clothes and his house, his wife and children, his ancestors and friends, his reputation and works, his lands and horses, and yacht and bank account. All
these things give him the same emotions. If they wax and prosper, he feels triumphant; if they dwin-
dle and die away, he feels cast down.

| REF. NO. 41 | See notes, pp. 148-151 | AUTHOR(S) | **William James** |

THE CONTENTED FISHERMAN

The rich industrialist from the North was horrified to find the Southern fisherman lying lazily beside his boat, smoking a pipe.

"Why aren't you out fishing?" said the industrialist.

"Because I have caught enough fish for the day," said the fisherman.

"Why don't you catch some more?"

"What would I do with it?"

"You could earn more money" was the reply. "With that you could have a motor fixed to your boat and go into deeper waters and catch more fish.

"Then you would make enough to buy nylon nets. These would bring you more fish and more money. Soon you would have enough money to own two boats...maybe even a fleet of boats. Then you would be a rich man like me."

"What would I do then?"

"Then you could really enjoy life."

"What do you think I am doing right now?"

REF. NO. 42)   **adapted from the original by Anthony de Mello**

2:12 PM -- The Deprivation Wage, or How to Avoid Profiting
from the Misfortune of Others

So on the one hand I've got folks nabbing the grail (or purporting to) without too much effort, who only serve to remind me how far I am from my own. How about these others, though? Whose jobs would seem to make an Eden of CS? And I don't have to cast too far for examples either, not with the accounting staff 20 yards from here, and sales right beside them. Just below me there's an actuarial consultancy I wouldn't join at gunpoint, and beneath them, an office full of patent lawyers, quiet as a morgue. You know what, forget it, I've got it made in CS.

Indeed, but even if I found myself down there plying all the life-affirming rules of patent and copyright, why couldn't I just lean out a window and have a look at those guys jackhammering the streets apart? That'd be a shot in the arm. Especially since after just a couple years of working a jackhammer, the ligaments holding your viscera in place start to attenuate and split like old elastics until you end up with your liver and pancreas and all that slipping into your lower abdomen and pooling there. Who knows, though, the guys in that crew might be thinking 'I know this sucks but it beats the hell out of mining coal or being that guy—the Great Waldo or Waldo the Great—who used to eat live mice off a plate in the basement of some Times Square burlesque house.' And for that matter, wouldn't Waldo have liked hearing about old Phineas Gage? The guy's dynamiting rocks for the old railroads, blows an iron spike up through his jaw and out the top of his head and rides an ox cart into town like that, the spike

The 'things could be worse' argument's a little more robust than this straw man of yours; see readings on p. 82.

still spitting his skull like a martini olive, gets it
pulled out and goes right back to work. That would have
cheered Waldo the Great up good.

Or probably not, any more than Waldo and his mice
help me through my shift in CS, any more than I'd start
beating my head on a wall just because it'd feel so
great to stop. But I hear that kind of advice anyway. My
problem is that I just don't know how good I've got it.
"If this was the Depression, son..."; "You might as easily have been born to build the Pyramids, you know."
Just situate your own job on a grand continuum of jobs
throughout history and you lose any grounds for complaint. A handy mental exercise that improves my station
in no way at all.

No one's saying life in CS is unacceptable. A damn
sight far from ideal, but not unacceptable. It's just that
the agreeability of this job, I've decided, may also be
its greatest hidden danger. I make a livable wage, I can
afford to rent a decent apartment, get a sampling of
those things a young adult would want from life. And as
estranged a notion as "pleasure" is from CS, the job has
its moments. I'm comfortable enough to put off a serious
job search indefinitely, which is why I'm not just going
nowhere fast, I'm actually going nowhere rather slowly.
Two years have gotten behind me already, and my most dramatic career move to date was that talk with John McKenna
at Mr. Hsu's. If I were working my days in a coal mine
(or slaughterhouse, tollbooth, door-to-door, etc.) I'd
damn well be working on my resume at night. At least I'd
be sure the position was temporary. Not so here.

So how much longer before I give in and learn to
accept my okay job, reconcile myself to an okay
lifestyle, to arguments like 'things could be a lot
worse than this'? I'm confronted with the image of
myself in this same cube 10 years from now, short-
sleeved oxford and tight perm like Lon's, the two of
us chumming around and taking lunches together, sipping
at the same malted with different straws in some
'50's-style soda fountain....

"Better to be a poor servant of a poor master, and to endure anything, rather than think as they do and live after their manner."
Homer

— quoted in Plato's Republic.

81

> Infirmity alone makes us take notice and learn, and enables us to analyse processes which we would otherwise know nothing about. A man who falls straight into bed every night, and ceases to live until the moment when he wakes and rises, will surely never dream of making, not necessarily great discoveries, but even minor observations about sleep. He scarcely knows that he is asleep. A little insomnia is not without its value in making us appreciate sleep, in throwing a ray of light upon that darkness. An unfailing memory is not a very powerful incentive to study the phenomena of memory.

REF. NO. 43)   *See notes, pp. 148-151*   AUTHOR(S)   **Marcel Proust**

> Here we have the second tragedy of happiness: people adapt to their circumstances, good or bad, the way their eyes adapt to sun or darkness. From that neutral point, improvement is happiness, loss is misery.

REF. NO. 44)   *See notes, pp. 148-151*   AUTHOR(S)   **Steven Pinker**

2:45 PM -- Hijinx

> The privilege of absurdity; to which no living creature is subject but man only.
>
> Thomas Hobbes

Sunlight comes to my corner of the office in the form of a single white disc no larger than a half dollar that makes a kind of celestial passage across the eastern wall of my cube, and whose brilliance and definition can, on days like today, be laser-like. It appears at 11:15 in the morning and moves 3 or 4 inches an hour, growing slowly more ovular in its transit, until about 4:30 when it vanishes abruptly. I've positioned a postcard of Elvis Presley and President Nixon so that at noon on the vernal equinox the beam falls right on their clasped hands, or it did last year anyhow. At 1:30 it becomes practical to bounce the sun ray off my watch crystal at passersby or, if I'm standing, at Maria in the cube adjoining mine to the left.

Now, in Maria's emotional repertoire there's mild irritation and acute irritation and that's about it. So this probably isn't a fantastic idea, but here I am doing it anyway. And I'm not playing around today either, I go right for the corner of her eye. She takes a little longer than you'd think to register it, then her face gets all pinched in. I'm nosing over

the wall to her cube looking good
and dopey. "You (which sounds like
hyou) are a very mature young man,"
I'm informed. Maria's cube looks
like some kind of Meso-American
notions shop.

"I'm a...I'm so mature, Maria,
that I pronounce the word 'mah-
toor.' Like I would say premah-
toor."

"No, you are a strange leedle
man. Why doan you leave me alone
and go play wid your clacker."
Nothing lewd here, she means the
Clacker, proper noun. Right, the
Clacker—let no man call Mark
Thornton a stranger to office buf-
foonery:

Jen Timmons came down with mono
some time back, I'm guessing early
spring, and took about a month and
a half on the bench. The company
with a heart sent her something
called the 'Barrel of Fun,' or they
were going to before the hot water
pipes burst over accounting and
everyone forgot about Jen's mono.
They didn't get around to posting
it until a few days before she
came back. She ended up bringing it
into work with her, unopened.

Well, the Barrel of Fun lived
right up to its name, first in
that it really was a little plastic
barrel, an exciting opalescent
jade-colored one, that opened on a
hinge. But more importantly, whoever'd made the thing had indeed
filled it to brimming with all manner of fun. Word-jumbles and cross-
word puzzles, a candy necklace and
red licorice whips, one of those

Workplace
Rebellion!

Whole lotta rebellion:
— Nose-ear pierce w/ chain
— Regulation necktie worn as
  belt
— Pilfer supplies (hardware,
  clocks, furniture)
— Indulge chew/dip habit at
  desk
— Disconnect client/mgr. phone
  call under pretext of trans-
  fer/hold
— Abstain from team/corp meetings

Armchair rebellion:
— Goatee, navel pierce
— Heavy-metal tee under standard-
  issue 50/50 oxford
— Pilfer supplies (software, sta-
  pler, mousepad)
— Solo cigarette breaks in hall-
  way/canteen
— Post-hangup epithets or unchari-
  table remarks for client/mgr.
— Theatrical inattention at
  team/corp meetings

Management-friendly "rebellion":
— Junior-senior TQM switcheroo (see
  10:45 TQM mtg.)
— Foment team 'rivalries' in race
  toward production targets
— "90 min. lunch hour" theater:
  training/institutional videos
— NCAA final-four gambling pool
— "Plaid day"

quiz books you write in with a special marker to make the answers appear, sunglasses and a Hot Wheels dragster, a glow-in-the-dark menagerie and a king's ransom in plastic jewels. The more fun we drew from the barrel, the more that seemed to remain. And Jen shared freely, allowing us to sample it all and take away those items that pleased us the most.

I came by late in the affair, to find the Barrel of Fun pretty well cashed. Still made off with a plastic box-like item, though, that nobody'd bothered to pull from its sleeve. No hints as to what it was save for a handle poking out with a lively arrangement of letters on it stating "The Clacker," in a way that kind of ripped off the Coca-Cola logo (see Figure III.5). With a few tentative shakes I found it would create, with minimal human help, a sharp, horse-hoof type report, unbearably loud. Which turned out to be the "toy's" lone *raison d'être*.

My discovery was followed immediately by the sensation of time loss. I can recall studying the Clacker...and...then coming to in another part of my cube with some of my files on the floor and my shirt untucked. The Clacker would be missing but I'd find where I dropped it, pick it up and begin again: I'd clack that damn thing for twenty minutes if I picked it up at all. I couldn't get enough. Whackawhackawhacka, loud as you please. I mean, someone had actually designed this, and someone else had included it in a Barrel of Fun. I couldn't stand it.

There were complaints, naturally. Even clients wanted to know what that racket was in the background. I'd tell them it was just the Clacker, and no one seemed to need any more information than that. A call went in to administration, of course, which brought Traci Vendler to my cube, long disappointed-matron face in full effect, palm held out for the Clacker. I surrendered it equally, glad as anyone to be rid of it. She inspected it and, I like to think, admired it. "Mark Thornton," she said, "your fun-time with this little...machine is officially over." Then she darted out.

I took off after her but she's pretty fleet. By the time I caught up she'd already dropped it out a transom window, 9 stories down into an alley. She told me "You are in an office. People are working here." I thought about that and said, "You're the one who bought it." (And the one who, inexplicably, had called it a 'machine.') She harumphed and went off to lunch.

Now, I know our interns are here to learn the biz and make connections, I know they represent a valuable company asset and we're only supposed to

set them on tasks of maximum mutual benefit. So was there something wrong with my sending Gary, whose family sank $23,000 into
this year's tuition, in part for him to be working with us, down
into that alley after the Clacker? Absolutely not. Took him all
of 10 minutes to locate the thing and bring it back to my desk,
perfectly intact.

I thanked Gary and set the Clacker by my phone, waited for
Traci to come back from lunch. She did and I waited still. Gave
her about 15 minutes to settle in, then started dialing. When
Traci picked up I clacked that goddamned thing into the receiver
with everything I had for about 30 seconds and hung up.

The following morning it was gone again, no matter. I gave
Gary a masterpiece of a peer review for his work in the field.
And I asked him on his last day what he thought
he'd learned here, this was back in June. He was
packing his effects into an army-style duffel.
He gave me all this party-line nonsense and I
listened patiently, then asked more specifically, what had he learned from hunting through the
Congress Street alley after the Clacker, as if
there'd been some secret point to it. He paused,
holding a pewter coffee coaster over the mouth
of the bag. "Umm, was that about persevering
with things? With not giving up until you finish
a job?" I pointed to him like you do in that
game 'charades,' like he'd guessed it exactly.

Fig. III.6
Natural state
of The Clacker

Involved here also is a certain inversion of the concept of wasted time. For the use-oriented, purposeful, need-reducing kind of person that time is wasted that achieves nothing and serves no purpose. While this is a perfectly legitimate usage, we may suggest that an equally legitimate usage
might be to consider that time wasted that does not carry end experience with it, that is, that is not
ultimately enjoyed. "Time that you enjoy wasting is not wasted time." "Some things that are not necessary may yet be essential."

An excellent illustration of the way in which our culture is unable to take its end experiences
straight may be seen in strolling, canoeing, golfing, and the like. Generally these activities are extolled
because they get people into the open, close to nature, out into the sunshine, or into beautiful sur-
roundings. In essence, these are ways in which what *should* be unmotivated end activities and end
experiences are thrown into a purposeful, achieving, pragmatic framework in order to appease the
Western conscience.

REF. NO. 45)   *See notes, pp. 148-151*   AUTHOR(S)   **Abraham Maslow**   85

3:02 PM -- American Dream: Friend or Foe?

In the square outside our building they've erected a monument to Samuel Adams that I have to pass twice a day. He's out there in all kinds of weather, heroically, oblivious as I slink past his feet. Those big-buckled dandy's shoes are arrested mid-stride as he treads some Colonial vista, one hand on a sword hilt and the other clutching a scroll that they'd have you believe is the Declaration of Independence (like he was allowed to walk around with it), the brow that presided over the fate of nations remaining knit today, apparently, with that responsibility. The legend reads: "Samuel Adams (1722-1803), Patriot and Statesman, Hero of the Revolutionary War, He Organized the Revolution and Signed the Declaration of Independence," the implication being "Now what have _you_ done?" And every day as I pass, bearing literally and metaphorically all the meaningless baggage of my workaday life, I have to return the same answer: nothing, not yet.

In customer service what I do is shuttle other people's work around. I oversee and explain and expedite. I do not produce things like ads or annual reports, or even the film to make these things. I don't erect buildings or plant trees, I don't assemble cars or teach anyone anything. I don't fight viruses or poverty for anyone but myself. I create things like information pipelines and the illusion of competence. I 'create' the happy customer. These don't count.

So what is the legacy of the CS lifer? Where do I take my kids to show them what I've spent my life working at? There won't be an exhibit or a movie, a bar or highway or grocery store that I'll be able to claim, people won't be doing any dance I've invented or reading my column. No one's going to write my biography or 'spot' me at a restaurant—if you've heard of me, you must be one of my clients. I'm looking ahead to the part when my first grader brings me in to explain my job to his or her peers, and I'm seeing a lot of fidgeting kids. I'm being asked by the teacher if I couldn't have just made something up.

If...you acquire a living knowledge of the history of great men, you will learn from it a supreme commandment: to become mature and to flee from that paralyzing upbringing of the present age which sees its advantage in preventing your growth so as to rule and exploit you to the full while you are still immature.

| REF. NO. 46 | _See notes, pp. 148-151_ | AUTHOR(S) **Friedrich Nietzsche** |

I think we're born to, and allowed for too long to indulge, an impractically high standard for measuring our own success. There isn't a 10-year-old in this country who doesn't plan on running it some day, or playing in a stadium-rock band or in the NFL or whatever it is that kids want. And they're not just <u>dreaming</u> of doing these things, is the point, they're <u>planning</u> on it. The challenge is only to decide, and there's no rush on that either. You may not even know what you want, but it awaits you nonetheless on the threshold of maturity.

Now, common sense will, in theory, introduce itself before you're ready for the workplace. Old notions of destiny will be challenged and made to survive on their plausibility; ambitions will divide neatly between the realistic and the illusory, and the latter will be (though not always painlessly) discarded. Surely no one graduates college still clinging to those fool lush-life notions of childhood...?

Except, well, I did. Or at least I didn't graduate thinking: *Now I'm going to work the phones for two years in an industry I don't even know exists yet, and afterward be no better off than when I started, in any measurable way.* It was more like: *No motivated grad need despair though s/he should first land in the mailroom: between those talents you were born with and the ones you've acquired, you'll quickly have boardroom doors swinging wide. And if problems of conscience should keep you from the corporate seats of power, there's room in Hollywood, and lots more of course in Africa...*

In 18 humbling months of customer service, I've had plenty of time, and cause, to revise the old assumptions, stretch out the old timelines. Which is a process, I realize, that ought to have been well underway in college. And the thing is it might have been, were it not for the infectious attitudes of two groups of people there—the career academics and the moneyed class—who are important enough to consider in turn:

The Setup, Part 1 -- Education...or is it?

Jason Pitcher co-edits a 'zine called "Can't, Won't," a morose opinion
paper that takes unflinching looks at various things. Here's a page from
their fall "Back to School" Number:

it, and there I am at a decent liberal-arts college
where I'm serving out a four-year sentence. Why
am I here? Because everyone goes to college,
because you don't get anywhere without a bachelor's
degree, because when you finish high school this is
what you must do. In an age when we complain of
mounting uncertainty, these have become unas-
sailable givens. Your parents will pay whatever is
demanded by way of tuition, you will help foot this
outrageous bill if instructed to do so, you will
accrue debts that will chase you like the Furies into
adulthood, you will struggle to outdo your peers in
pleasing the spokespeople of the intelligentsia, so-
called, you will accept and show enthusiasm for
whatever counter-culture ethos is in place among
students, you will encounter lurid extremes of ser-
vility and pomposity, you will submit to the fugitive
standards of competence held by an embittered
collection of graduate-student teaching fellows,
you will render opinions that you'll wrongly imagine hold great weight for society, you will be
encouraged to challenge yourself and others but
only in a way that the academics deem acceptable.
And you'll be thrust into the job market completely
unendowed, save for the wits you came to college
with (give or take), a handful of connections, what
social aplomb you've learned from colleagues, and
what value the reputation of your college carries
with your interviewers. The cost? $50-$100,000
and four years of your life, good ones. Ask any

· 17 ·

88

And it goes on in this vein for some time. Much of which coincides with my opinion and experience though I don't "live," as does Pitcher, "to see my alma mater burn." He's phrasing, in typical blood-and-thunder fashion, the kind of blanket complaint you hear from anyone who got bushwhacked in his or her first foray out of college.

For me the liberal arts sham wasn't a sham exactly, it was just a program that misfired. What's curious is that it did so with every appearance of intentionality. The image is this: an unwitting kid is being equipped and sent off to battle by his eccentric grandparents. All the 'necessities' of war are being heaped on him affectionately and with no doubts about their someday utility: here's your bonnet and parasol, your Britannica, your slide-rule and concertina, some eggnog and ribbon-candy and quinine, let's see...take this heavy and handleless trunk but don't open it till you get back, and oh, now, this is an original Gauguin, if this is lost or in any way besmirched you'll live to regret it.... If the elder couple are veterans at all it's of some stillborn campaign, long-ago and disastrous; and by now what memories might have served as a practical guide have been scoured away or rendered bizarre by the intervening years. Nor would they claim otherwise. Still the kid's trust in his grandparents' foreknowledge is implicit, as is their faith in their own lights. This is, after all, how they'd be equipping themselves if they were young and foolhardy enough to have another go at it.

Just so with the academicians. It becomes a point of pride, the inutility of that academic baggage. If you want to learn a trade, they'll proclaim in as many words, then go to a trade school; if you want to be prepared for life, which may or may not presume a career, you'll stay put and keep reading. Instructors have a four-year-long opportunity to freight their students with knowledge that, unlike post-graduation learning, is free from any constraint of practicality. So why make it practical? Much better to pack everyone a basket of delights for the intellect. Every kid's going to learn the barbarous and mundane rules of work and life and success soon enough, so why sully the experience of pure learning when this may be its final stand? An instructor with access to a hundred thousand volumes, many self-authored, should devise a curriculum that any half-wit manager could, and will, just as easily deliver? I should say not.

It all makes a queer kind of sense, too, like TQM in the conference room, or 'creative exchange' in Mara's living room, working within the right set of givens. Step outside though, graduate, and you're left right where you should have known you'd be, with the knowledge that you're going to have to figure this out for yourself. That's what I ought to have appreciated sooner, and might have if I weren't convinced in college that there'd be nothing more difficult or important in life than completing my education—not that college seemed overwhelmingly important or difficult, even at the time, but everything afterward was supposed to be even less so.

A number of students began mulling their career options long before that final June, I remember, but most of us still regarded graduation as a kind of spiritual death (the whole 'commencement' idea aside). As with real death, no one knew what it would entail, yet we were encouraged not to fret the abyss for though it might not be preferable to the academic life, it would at least be a great deal easier. You were going to set a goal and work toward it. Simple. You may have to work hard but at least there won't be any distractions like a capella singing groups, build-your-own armillary spheres or the War of the Roses. Single-mindedness will suddenly become an option.

So the idea corroborated, if not authored, by the career academics was this: there's nothing tricky about rising through the corporate ranks, massing a fortune, distinguishing yourself in your vocation. Not at least compared to the rigors of academia. In fact, should you retain the lessons of your college education you'll find it difficult to avoid success. Success in the workplace was not just a foregone certainty for the desirous graduate but, in the opinion of some instructors, an ignominious cop-out....

The cruel lesson is that there's no longer a place in the world for that time-honored college product, the academic dilettante. Not at least in the workplace. Go in spouting Shelley and Herodotus and you'll not only fail to impress your coworkers and peers, you'll anger them. The knowledge you'd thought to call on to distinguish yourself here has become extraneous; with nowhere to apply them, your lessons become these comically anguished old ghosts, rattling their chains with fast-diminishing fury. The idea that you'd be responsible for carrying the so-called cultural capital, the intellectual *noblesse oblige*, is now only a source of guilt, a relinquishing of your own trumped-up ideas of potential.

And if that weren't disheartening enough, stepping from that halcyon college daydream into a dead-end job like mine and held down there with no discernible out, you also find you've been labeled spoiled, useless, feckless by middle-age media cranks, who seem to hold great sway with bosses and parents and most of the other stewards of society and commerce. What the young generation needs, I'm told, is a grand project (a new expression for 'swift kick in the pants'), like a war or a depression. Some kind of challenge to 'smite the mind rigid.' Then we'd lay off this introspective folderol and get busy....

That is, regarding your responsibilities as a bearer of cultural capital:

don't take it too seriously. The academic noblesse oblige, as you've phrased it (tongue-in-cheek, we suspect), has always been a subject of ridicule.

In the past decade or so the American people have developed a very unhealthy attitude toward the concept of failure. Basically, they have stopped loathing it. In certain situations, they have begun to admire it. And in a limited number of horrifying scenarios, they are actually taking steps to reward it....

The culture of failure can be seen at its most insidious in the way we are raising our children. Where once public schools viewed their mission as the grounding of youngsters in reading, writing, and 'rithmetic, they now passionately devote themselves to raising students' self-esteem. The result is dumbed-down SAT tests, absurdly generous grading, report cards that mean absolutely nothing. The result is a generation of young people who can't read, can't count, can't speak foreign languages, can't think. But who nevertheless feel pretty good about themselves.

REF. NO. 49) *See notes, pp. 148-151* **AUTHOR(S)** **Joe Queenan**

Queenan supplies an example of the generation-bashing you refer to, this one in an article called "Failure Chic;" Botstein and Whitehead weigh in on the other side of the debate:

If there really had been such a good school system in the past, the adult world would not leave so much to be desired.

The issue, therefore, is not how to reclaim virtue lost, but how to make the present and future better than the past. As far as education is concerned, the cultural pessimism that has become so popular and commonplace is the most difficult obstacle to overcome. The motivation of any child, whether four years of age or fourteen, is dependent on a sense of optimism around that child. No generation of American children has ever gone to school surrounded by adults—from parents to teachers—who as a group believed so overwhelmingly in the inevitability of decline.

REF. NO. 50) *See notes, pp. 148-151* **AUTHOR(S)** **Leon Botstein**

. . . .

The great educational tragedy of our time is that many American children are failing school not because they are intellectually or physically impaired but because they are emotionally incapacitated. [T]eachers find many children emotionally distracted, so upset and preoccupied by the explosive drama of their own family lives that they are unable to concentrate on such mundane matters as multiplication tables.

In response, many schools have turned to therapeutic remediation. A growing proportion of many school budgets is devoted to counseling and other psychological services. The curriculum is becoming more therapeutic; children are taking courses in self-esteem, conflict resolution, and aggression management.... Schools are increasingly becoming emergency rooms of the emotions, devoted not only to developing minds but also to repairing hearts. As a result, the mission of the school, along with the culture of the classroom, is slowly changing. What we are seeing, largely as a result of the new burdens of family disruption, is the psychologization of American education.

REF. NO. 51) **AUTHOR(S)** **Barbara Dafoe Whitehead**

I always believed that at some time fate would take from me the terrible effort and duty of educating myself: I believed that, when the time came, I would discover a philosopher to educate me, a true philosopher whom one could follow without any misgiving because one would have more faith in him than one had in oneself. Then I asked myself: what would be the principles by which he would educate you?—and I reflected on what he might say about the two educational maxims which are being hatched in our time. One of them demands that the educator should quickly recognize the real strength of his pupil and then direct all his efforts and energy and heat at them so as to help that one virtue to attain true maturity and fruitfulness. The other maxim, on the contrary, requires that the educator should draw forth and nourish all the forces which exist in his pupil and bring them to a harmonious relationship with one another.

REF. NO. 52 | *See notes, pp. 148-151* | AUTHOR(S) | **Friedrich Nietzsche**

I would have wished for him, the one wise custodian of the truth, to tell me what I ought rightly to think of Shakespeare, of Saintine, of Sophocles, of Euripides, of Silvio Pellico.... Above all, I would have wished him to tell me whether I would have had a better chance of arriving at the truth by repeating my first-form year at school, or by becoming a diplomat, or a barrister at the Court of Appeal.

REF. NO. 53 | *See notes, pp. 148-151* | AUTHOR(S) | **Marcel Proust**

If the colleges were better, if they really had it, you would need to get the police at the gates to keep order in the inrushing multitude. See in college how we thwart the natural love of learning by leaving the natural method of teaching what each wishes to learn, and insisting that you shall learn what you have no taste or capacity for. The college, which should be a place of delightful labor, is made odious and unhealthy, and the young men are tempted to frivolous amusements to rally their jaded spirits. I would have the studies elective. Scholarship is to be created not by compulsion, but by awakening a pure interest in knowledge. The wise instructor accomplishes this by opening to his pupils precisely the attractions the study has for himself. The marking is a system for schools, not for the college; for boys, not for men; and it is an ungracious work to put on a professor.

REF. NO. 54 | AUTHOR(S) | **attributed to Ralph Waldo Emerson**

As might be expected, such a position has certain implications for helping us to understand why conventional education in this country falls so far short of its goals. We shall stress only one point here, namely, that education makes little effort to teach individuals to examine reality directly and freshly. Rather it gives them a complete set of prefabricated spectacles with which to look at the world in every aspect, such as what to believe, what to like, what to approve of, what to feel guilty about. Rarely is each person's individuality made much of, rarely is he or she encouraged to be bold enough to see reality in his or her own style, or to be iconoclastic or different. Proof for the contention of stereotyping in higher education can be obtained in practically any college catalog, in which all of shifting, ineffable, and mysterious reality is neatly divided into three credit slices which, by some miraculous coincidence, are exactly 15 weeks long, and which fall apart neatly, as a tangerine does, into completely independent and mutually exclusive departments. If ever there was a perfect example of a set of categories imposed *upon* reality rather than *by* reality, this is it.

REF. NO. 55 | *See notes, pp. 148-151* | AUTHOR(S) | **Abraham Maslow**

Can't say you're the first person to feel misdirected or short-changed by your educational experience.

<u>The Setup, Part 2 -- Playing with the Players</u>

Here the image is a group of lemmings, spirited and heedless, running
along toward the edge of a seaside precipice. When they reach it, they
all, impossibly, take wing, save for the real lemming, the flightless
one, who falls to his death.

I stayed aloft for exactly two days after graduating, and then I went
to work at an express picture-frame shop, where more than one of my colleagues showed up, aghast, as customers. What on earth was I doing here?
Well I was making money, so I could do things like eat and pay rent.
Seven months there, followed by a string of temp jobs that would eventually drop me here. But I'm still reeling from that crash-landing in the
frame store, hobbling from the wreck it had made of my expectations.

Like I say, I learned part of what made a natural phase change into
cataclysm from my college instructors. The other part came from absorbing
the behaviors and presumptions of well-to-do peers.

These were people who could rightly indulge dreams of corporate gov-
ernance, and think of leisure in terms large-scale and exotic. I hung
out with them and got to thinking, yeah, that's for me. I seemed to be
presented with that same array of post-graduation options: want to take
some time off, travel, gather your wits? want to intern around at a few
different companies, reconnoiter, see what grabs you? want to start a
company of your own? would you consider, if need be, the family business? taking the reins from your parents? The truth was that none of
this was going to be effortless, not even for them. Work-world miscon-
ceptions run roughshod through every campus in the country, and that's
nothing new; we were all in for some surprises. But there's a difference
between reorienting and crash-landing--it's the difference between grad
schools or internships and FrameWerks XPress.

Here are two things I'd have done well to figure out sooner: first of
all, the rich kids I knew weren't rich, their parents were, are. And family fortunes don't just get unearthed while dad's digging in the yard.
The accumulation of fortune is an arduous, difficult, often unsavory business. That's the second-of-all: the ease and glamour of the moneyed
lifestyle is only its public face (again, how could I not have known
this?). In the main these are people who've inherited, or worked their
way up in, the unheard-of industries. They mill ball-bearings or agricul-
tural machinery, they run parking lot empires and flea market chains.
Somewhere behind the machine that crimps the ends of metal toothpaste and
ointment tubes is some hard-bitten Midas with places in Manhattan and
Aspen, maybe Key West and Capri too, and somewhere a son or daughter of
his is planning a graduation trip to the Greek Islands and considering a
career in kinetic sculpture. The father of a college friend of mine

patented those reflector barrels they plant around highway construction, some time in the early 1970's. Then what did he do for 25 years? Sell his barrels. By the time he had a son in college, the man was rich as Croesus. And the son's in venture capital now, helping stake the entrepreneurial ventures of other wealthy people's sons and daughters.

So back to me, present-day, slouching past Samuel Adams on my way to work. With no reflector barrel king in the family tree, and no succor from any college reading or lesson remembered. Just day after day of Lon and customer service. Sam Adams Organized a Revolution and Governed a Commonwealth, for Christ's sake, and what have I done? Nothing, not yet.

Tell you what I won't do, though, is sink 25 years of my life into selling highway barrels. I don't even think I'd get much of a kick out of managing venture capital. And as for staying where I am—again the image of Lon and me, pompadours, sipping on malteds—forget that, too.

It's not as though I need fortune or celebrity or anything on an earth-jarring scale, I can live with plenty of my desires and even needs going unfulfilled, I don't want to lead the nation anywhere or die leaving a smoking crater in place of some city. But how about a job that's bringing material and spiritual reward in some kind of profusion, not without, but maybe in a sensible proportion to, the labor going in? Sounds modest enough, as aspirations go. But in terms of adding details to my vision of the future, it isn't worth much. It's so broad—what does it mean, specifically? I'm sure there's material and spiritual reward to be taken from any of a thousand jobs, but that seems to be part of the problem: with so many options for the future none of them seem outstanding in any way. There are so many paths crossing the same ground, they've all grown ill-defined.

At the same time, the images of success, people enjoying success, are everywhere, lifestyles touted in fact and fiction, paraded right past me but flying, like shades through the hands of the living, whenever I so much as think of bridging the distance between here and there. And while that tantalization might foster what we call ambition, its by-product, or residue, is a restlessness so vast and tireless it's like an elemental force.

Welcome to the American Dream of the spoiled, the useless, the feckless. It's impetus without direction, a longing as formless and unrequitable as it is stubborn. It's about having 'more,' certainly, but that's all I can pin to it. Don't know what I want or how to get it, but I'll know when I've got it, is the idea.

So friend or foe, the American Dream? It's a ward against stagnation, and it's helpful in that way. I doubt very much, for instance, that I'll be seeing out another year in CS. The American Dream may even pave the road to success, once I figure out how to harness it properly. But in the meantime, it seems to have given failure a dangerously high likelihood and cost.

Refer back to p. 77, first couple of lines from Peter Drucker, or to Barbara Sher's book, I Could Do Anything If I Only Knew What It Was. Overabundance of freedom or choice may not be an unqualified boon.

94

Pellerin used to read every book on aesthetics he could lay his hands on, in the hope of discovering the true theory of Beauty, for he was convinced that once he had found it he would be able to paint masterpieces. He surrounded himself with every conceivable accessory—drawings, plaster casts, models, engravings—and hunted around fretfully, blaming the weather, his nerves or his studio, going out into the street to seek inspiration, thrilling with joy when he had found it, but then abandoning the work he had begun, to dream of another which would be even finer. Tortured by a longing for fame, wasting his days in argument, believing in countless ridiculous ideas, in systems, in criticisms, in the importance of the codification or reform of art, he had reached the age of fifty without producing anything but sketches.

REF. NO. 56) *See notes, pp. 148-151*   AUTHOR(S)   **Gustave Flaubert**

Flaubert, on the self-defeating properties of ambition.

Nor is the time pressure as great as you might imagine (refer also to list on p. 86).

[H]ave patience with everything that remains unsolved in your heart. Try to love the *questions themselves*, like locked rooms and like books written in a foreign language. Do not now look for the answers. They cannot now be given to you because you could not live them. It is a question of experiencing everything. At present you need to *live* the question. Perhaps you will gradually, without even noticing it, find yourself experiencing the answer, some distant day.

REF. NO. 57) *See notes, pp. 148-151*   AUTHOR(S)   **Rainer Maria Rilke**

Our vocation is not a sphinx's riddle, which we must solve in one guess or else perish. Some people find, in the end, that they have made many wrong guesses and that their paradoxical vocation is to go through life guessing wrong. It takes them a long time to find out that they are happier that way.

REF. NO. 58) *See notes, pp. 148-151*   AUTHOR(S)   **Thomas Merton**

Pellerin, after dabbling in Fourierism, homoeopathy, table-turning, Gothic art, and humanitarian painting, had become a photographer; and on all the walls of Paris there were pictures of him in a black coat, with a tiny body and a huge head.

REF. NO. 59) *See notes, pp. 148-151*   AUTHOR(S)   **Gustave Flaubert**

It doesn't happen all at once...you become. It takes a long time.   **Margery Williams**

3:16 PM -- Steve Schimmer: Voice of the Herd

Workplace fallacy: Everyone Applauds Initiative. This isn't just naive thinking, it invites trouble.

I ought to have prepared some elaborate cover-up for this journal, where I'm doing parts of it on company time. There are too many people with too little range, who'd go out of their way to expose or sabotage something like this. It's unconventional, so it'll excite the curiosity, and then the jealousy or anger or derision, of certain other employees. One of them being Steve Schimmer who, appearing outside my cubicle at 3:15, can see that I'm writing in a journal instead of manning my computer or the phone like everyone else. And though the serendipity of our encounter seems genuine, this was the visit I should have counted on. There's nothing, after all, that attracts the meddlesome coworker like incongruity.

Steve announces himself by lurking in your peripheral vision until you're forced to register him. It's a habit of his that I really have no patience for. And for my added pleasure today, he's gnawing his way through an apple, mouth wide open, natch. He just

stands there behind my right ear, hanging an elbow on the
divider wall, his mouth a wet percussion orchestra of sloshing
and smacking, like a washing machine left open.

"Afternoon Steve," I say without looking up.

"Thornton. Doing some writing," is what he says. Here's the
sort of guy who'll see you lugging groceries and say: 'Se-eww,
you going shopping, buddy?'

"Appears that way."

"Can I ask what it is you're writing, then?" <u>Chomp</u> on the
apple.

"Ah, sure you can."

"Oka-ay," as if he's talking to a drunkard or an attentive
animal, "what is it you're writing there, Mark?"

"Actually it's just notes, I'm not <u>writing</u> anything until
later, it's...hard to explain." No point in making this easy
for him. He sighs through his nose and deposits himself on my
guest chair, motioning with what's left of his apple at my
wastebasket, hidden under a counter, until I tilt it out for
him. Then he steals a last bite and flings it in. "Buries it!"
he exclaims. I wait a spell. Steve draws his glasses from a
breast pocket and starts burnishing the lenses with his tie.

"Heard something about a kind of day-on-the-job thing
you're writing," he sez, easy as a month in the country.

Fine. He knows. I'll just run through this as quickly as I
can, try not to sound defensive, brace for whatever he's been
waiting to say about it. He inspects his fingernails, nips at
one or two as I'm talking. When I'm done, he drags the back of
his hand across his lips.

"Well. How many days are you getting off for this?"

"I'm not getting any. I get one day to work at about 90%
capacity while I take notes, that's today, and one day to
organize and expand on whatever I've written, but I have to
prepare the rest of the journal on my own time. And when I get
it back from the people annotating it, the people at SysCorp,
I have to write Senior Management a summation brief, to evalu-
ate the process and tell them what I learned."

"That's what those notes are, you're keeping a journal? Why
are you calling it a journal?"

"Because that's what it is, it's a personal record of
events, and observations, I just happen to be keeping it on a
workday. What would you call it?"

"An excuse to get off work, I'd call it." Smug laughter. "So

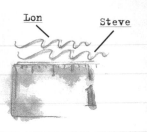

Fig. III.7

Kinks per inch,
Lon v. Steve Schimmer

you're keeping a journal of a typical day's work"--uh-huh--"which somebody is then going to read and make comments on"--uh-huh--"and return to you with some passages they think you'll find...illuminating?" Uh-huh. He fixes me over the top of his glasses.

"Yeah, I have to do it for TQM," I say, like it's a huge imposition. He'll leave me alone if I can convince him I'm suffering. Schimmer goes scratching in his hair with a couple apple-slicked fingers. That hair of his is as angrily kinked as Lon's but longer, unreasonably long, with this used-up or corrupted look as though it were the outward extension of some inner ferment.

"Se-ew, if you're doing it as a part of TQM, ahh, how come no one else is doing it?"

I give that one a shrug, essaying boredom. "I dunno, I was the one who'd heard about it first, thought the program sounded cool and I ran it past Senior Management. I'm the lab rat for now, if the program works for me they'll pay for everyone to do it...."

"Don't be offended, Mark," a malevolent smile forming, "but I think this is idiotic."

"Well, of course you do."

"We-hell, what do we mean by that remark, Mark?" He cocks his head playfully and adds: "Remarkmark?"

What I don't say is this:

Point is, Steve, you labor long enough under the same assumptions, you guard them assiduously enough, and you grow unable or unwilling to make allowances for other ways of doing things. Never mind that this is just one in an infinite number of real and potential corporate universes. You come in, you work your job and push slowly ahead, and then you leave. You represent what on the positive side is called contentment. You're deaf to any sirens that might be calling you off the course, questions of what am I doing here, how can I be happier, isn't there a better way of doing this. You're spared the agonies of self-doubt.

On the negative side, though, holding so fast to your givens has made you an enemy of novelty and uncertainty and nonlinear progress. Because these are things that threaten the status quo. To question your assumptions is also to imperil the corporate order--which makes an experiment like mine unthinkable, or in

your words, idiotic. Makes me a reckless deviant, a sower of dis-
content, who's looking to get slapped down....
   I might say something like that but I keep my counsel. Even if
I were in the mood to get into this with Steve, I'm not going to
convince him of anything. More likely he'd win me over to his way
of thinking.
   "Nothing, I don't mean anything by that" is what I end up saying, "just, of course this seems a little unorthodox. Does to me
too. Bet you can't wait to tell those goombahs of yours in
accounting."
   "Right, I guess I better get to that now."
   "Be sure to make me sound like a complete jackass, would you?"
   "Hey," he says down the angle of his shoulder, "I calls 'em
like I sees 'em."

Since Frederic's distress had no rational cause, and since he could not ascribe it to any actual misfortune, Martinon utterly failed to understand his lamentations about life.

REF. NO. 62) *See notes, pp. 148-151*   AUTHOR(S)   **Gustave Flaubert**

Where this disquiet of yours is neither bizarre nor unexampled, there will always be others
who'll have no grasp of what you're carrying on about, or who'll outright deny you the
grounds for complaint.

What I must do is all that concerns me, not what the people think. This rule, equally arduous in
actual and in intellectual life, may serve for the whole distinction between greatness and meanness.
It is the harder because you will always find those who think they know what is your duty better than
you know it. It is easy in the world to live after the world's opinion; it is easy in solitude to live after
our own; but the great man is he who in the midst of the crowd keeps with perfect sweetness the
independence of solitude.

REF. NO. 63) *See notes, pp. 148-151*   AUTHOR(S)   **Ralph Waldo Emerson**

. . . .

Men would say of him that up he went and down he came without his eyes; and that it was better
not even to think of ascending; and if any one tried to loose another and lead him up to the light, let
them only catch the offender, and they would put him to death.

REF. NO. 64) *See notes, pp. 148-151*   AUTHOR(S)   **Plato**

"Metal conducts heat, do not touch hot metal, learn your task quickly and repeat it flawlessly, keep your mouth shut and stay out of the union." Terrell screws a stamped-out White Owl into the corner of his mouth and addresses a panel of blackened drywall, where he's written the word Arc-weld in yellow chalk. What he says next, I don't remember, but I can recreate that lead-in first word to last. Rarely do you hear anyone make so much sense in so little time.

That kind of instruction is simple, practical and actually worth something. It can get you promoted, earn you money, and save your ass. Where I worked my summers in college, you needn't have taken anyone's word for anything: you could find out first-hand. Fail to ground yourself when you're fishing in a gearbox for a fallen part, and your central nervous system will light up like a pinball machine. I know because I did it. When the truth is so easily demonstrable, it breeds trust.

My most significant and memorable lesson in teamwork, for instance, came almost six years before TQM, in the machine shop. Went something like this:

"Listen to me. Pay attention to what you're doing and stop fucking up parts on your drill." My instructor, Pete Castine, was an inch taller and a foot broader than me, a formidable beer gut under his Charlie Daniels Band tee-shirt. His forearms were hocks of filthy muscle covered over in the grease and filings from the iron rails he cut for twelve hours a day downstairs.

"You fuck up parts and we don't get as many contracts, we don't get as many contracts and we got to tool down, we tool down and I don't get overtime and I don't work those hours and I don't get paid. Stop fucking up."

Then he balled his left fist, held it up for me to see (I remember the word LOVE tattooed across his fingers), and hit me square in the breadbox, knocking me back three steps and landing me flat on my ass on the shop floor. A bunch of guys were standing around and they thought this was a real gas. There's really no good way to handle that kind of scene so I just stood up and went back to work like nothing had happened, though that wallop stalled the air in my lungs for a good half hour.

I'd been at the shop for about two weeks and still didn't have the first idea about what I was doing. I knew three parts of mine in fifty went into the waste barrel but I figured what the hell, all I do is drill six holes in a piece of aluminum. I had no idea

what the thing did, and since I didn't do
piecework, I got paid no matter what.
Besides it was just for the summer. But my
conversation with Pete taught me something: whatever the hell that twenty pound
piece of metal did, ten guys had worked on
it by the time it hit me, and another
twelve would work on it afterward.

You could see the things lying around
the place stacked on pallets according to
where they were in the process. Some guys
held on to them for a while and ran each
one through a whole bunch of procedures.
Somebody downstairs had taken a flatfile
to all of their surfaces and angles until
there wasn't a single burr in a thousand
of them. Others, like me, handled each
piece for five minutes total. All I did
was drill three holes about an inch deep
in one end, turn it over and drill three
more in the exact same spots on the other
end. There was even a jig I put over the
ends and cinched into place that had the
holes all set for me. My hands got covered
in an oil that was yellow and smelled like
butter, the oil I'd slather over the bit
every time I ran a stroke on the drill.

Anyhow, after Pete knocked me on my ass
I realized what was happening every time I
threw one of those things in the barrel. I
was rendering worthless all the work that
the guys in front of me had done. And by
the time each piece reached me, it represented a substantial investment of labor.
Our shop turned thirty-foot lengths of
extruded aluminum gutter into a component with size tolerances of
ten one-thousandths of an inch (that's the thickness of two sheets
of notepaper) and fifty different holes drilled in its various
sides like the cooling jacket on a machine gun, tapped with threads
to hold metal plates on either end, with ten rods screwed in at
intervals along its length, the whole thing capped with a high con-
ductivity plate that made them strangely fragile and gave them a
yellowish luster.

Fig. III.8

Rich used to dole out
his "amino acid"
pills—which were real-
ly just crank—to his
friends at the machine
shop. When they start-
ed making me nauseous
I tossed them, but to
stay "in" with Rich I
still had to act like
I was speeding. I'd
be there in the lunch
room ready to col-
lapse, and he'd walk
in and I'd have to
start gnawing on my
fingernails and drum-
ming my feet on the
floor.

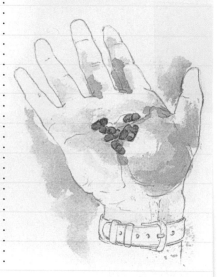

About a hundred hours of work went into each of these compo-
nents. We sold them to a phone company. The parts went out of the
shop and came back to us in the form of money, which we could use
to buy beer and cigarettes and tattoos, and to support families
if we had them, and to go back to college if we wanted. It all
got real simple for me. Work hard with a lot of people and make
something that someone will buy. Make a lot of them and make them
well so people trust you and want to buy more. Simple.

I started paying more attention to what I was doing, like you
would on any job where screwing up could get you hit. I started to
get more comfortable, even deft, with the drill. After that they
had me tapping the parts as well, a tricky operation where you put
in the threads that picked up a screw that in turn held a plate
over the component end. It's tough because the steel that taps are
made out of is really brittle and if you jar the part at all you can
snap it off like an icicle. After a month I was burying the next
three people in line and I still hadn't broken a tap. Guys started
making room for me at the sinks in the washroom. I went back summer
after summer and eventually they started using me as a floater and
trouble-shooter. I learned most of the machines in the place and got
put where we were backed up or where there were a lot of small parts
that had to be fit into a larger piece.

A quick side-note here, as I consider the machine shop. I'm not one
to romanticize manual labor, at all, but I think we really over-sell
the white collar package. A machine shop is not, we are told, any place
for the self-respecting college graduate...but think about it. Any
industrious grunt in the shop could support a family, own a house, a
car, a pair of dirtbikes or ATVs or snowmobiles or whatever--unthink-
able for a junior staffer here. Nor is there any of that salt-of-the-
earth honesty or vitality here, real or affected. Or any sense of that
macho confederacy, that pull-together drive of the assembly liner (even
if it was just the collusion you'd expect among hell's inmates). None
of that here, anyway, these cubes are designed to fragment our staff
and even if they weren't, we wouldn't have much to do with one another-
-that 'team' business aside, this is a lonely and dispiriting workday.
But that work we did in the shop, it was so...mindless, right? Sure,
but you could train dogs to do my job here too.

It's not an argument I give much thought to, just another aggra-
vating perspective on my current position. It helps to remember that
in the shop what I wanted most in the world was to get out. I even
looked forward to school, in the way Dante would have cast himself
into boiling glass to escape the fires of Purgatory.

But keeping strictly to employee management—and that was the original point—I think the machine shop model, primitive as it was, shouldn't be forsaken outright for TQM and the other products of management evolution, so-called. I owed, I realize, whatever proficiency I'd gained on those machines, and any cachet I'd won in the process, to my 30-second motivation tutorial with Pete. And that, less the violence, was the norm for work-related communication in the shop: cogent, practical, honest and direct. We would value and trust whatever thoughts Pete or Terrell or the other managers gave voice to. Got to think there's a lesson in here somewhere for Lon.

Lon Presents:
YOU Figure it Out.

Lon sez: "Well I'm not a full WASP, but I'm white and Anglo-Saxon, I'm just a Catholic. So I meet three of the four criteria."

Kendra sez: "Yeah Lon, but there are only three criteria total. Anglo-Saxon's one thing."

Lon sez, with 100% assurance: "I know that, I'm saying I'm THREE of the FOUR."

When I heard the learn'd astronomer,
When the proofs, the figures, were ranged in columns before me,
When I was shown the charts and diagrams, to add, divide, and measure them,
When I sitting heard the astronomer, where he lectured
    with much applause in the lecture-room,
How soon unaccountable I became tired and sick,
Till rising and gliding out I wander'd off by myself,
In the mystical moist night-air, and from time to time,
Look'd up in perfect silence at the stars.

REF. NO. 65 | AUTHOR(S) **Walt Whitman**

. . . .

The Roman rule was, to teach a boy nothing that he could not learn standing.... The sight of the planet through a telescope is worth all the course on astronomy: the shock of the electric spark in the elbow outvalues all the theories; the taste of the nitrous oxide, the firing of an artificial volcano, are better than volumes of chemistry.

REF. NO. 66 | AUTHOR(S) **Ralph Waldo Emerson**

If we seek work as nothing but an unpleasant necessity, it is no use talking about good work, unless we mean *less* work. Why put any goodness into our work beyond the absolute minimum? Who could afford to do good work? What would be the point of making something perfect when something imperfect would do as well? Ananda Coomaraswamy used to say: "Industry without art is brutality." Why? Because it damages the soul and spirit of the worker. He could say this only because his metaphysics is very different from that of the modern world. He also said: "It is not as if the artist were a special kind of man; every man is a special kind of artist." This is the metaphysics of good work.

REF. NO. 67 | *See notes, pp. 148-151* | AUTHOR(S) **E. F. Schumacher**

3:22 PM -- Memory Serves, Part 2: Running with the Giants and Losing

The situation in school was always a neat reverse of the machine shop. Everyone proving at great length why they should be listened to no more than some of the time. And just like the early tone-setting events in the shop have taken up permanent residence in my mind, so it was in school. Actually the seminal event is one of my earliest childhood memories:

Howie Dennison and I'd gotten around the alphabet pretty quickly in the first grade, which I doubt we'd have done if we'd foreseen the rewards of first-grade scholarship. We were plucked out of regular class and detained in the old remedial reading room opposite a chesty old-school disciplinarian named Miss Peyser. For one hour a day her job was to wave stack on stack of flashcards at us, each with a vocabulary word in hundred-point type, some with an equally-baffling 'clue' illustration on the reverse. They might have let us move on to sentences, but most of what I remember is a long and disjointed procession of words.

"Forth-right. Good Howie, now let Mark guess at the next one. Cau-ty-- oh, cautious. Good. Sal-a-ry. Good. Stomach, is that stomach ache? Yes it is," &c.

Up came the word recipe one day and we were sandbagged pretty good. Nor had Miss Peyser gotten an illus- trated clue to bail her out, so she started in with her Password routine. When we got to this stage she'd grow especially testy, and this was a woman given to wicked fits of temper anyway, even when things were going smoothly.

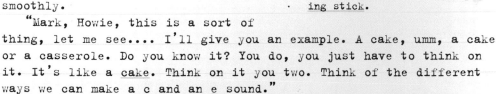

Fig III.9
Here's poor Stovepipe the Pelican with his clue for "Stomach ache." I remember this one because it really upset me. He's got his trademark hat and ruined carna- tion, the pince-nez and waistcoat and epaulettes. If his hands weren't clutching his stomach they'd be toting his candy-cane walk- ing stick.

"Mark, Howie, this is a sort of thing, let me see.... I'll give you an example. A cake, umm, a cake or a casserole. Do you know it? You do, you just have to think on it. It's like a cake. Think on it you two. Think of the different ways we can make a c and an e sound."

Well, the more I taxed myself, the less cakes and casseroles were having to do with that word, and Howie was just staring off. When she finally said "Recipe, this card says recipe, now write it down in your workbook," I'd had enough. Miss Peyser, I said, a cake isn't an example of a recipe, you use a recipe to *make* a cake. Same with a casserole. A recipe is like three eggs, a glass of milk, baking soda. A cake is not a recipe. Right?

Her eyes narrowed just a little. "No, no, Mark. The word is recipe. I think it's difficult for you because it has a soft c like the first c in circus, not hard like the second c in circus or the c in clown, which are hard c's. Recipe. Have you written it down yet? Howie has it written down already."

I said, Yes but a cake is not--

"Mark, please write it down in your workbook right now. A cake is a kind of recipe and so is a casserole, or a loaf of banana bread. You're familiar with cake and banana bread, aren't you." I just said yes, Miss Peyser, and wrote it down in my workbook like I had seen Howie do.

3:30 PM -- One More Reason Never to Leave my Cube: Clay Pirner

I'm headed out of the employee lounge with a paper cup o' company joe, the bottom already sodden through, when here comes Clay Pirner, our head of sales. What's going on, Clay?

"I'm cashin' checks and snappin' necks. Same's always. What's your story, Thornton?" He stops in front of me in that wishbone-legged stance, rubbing his palms together, superstar grin looming a good 6 inches over the top of my head. Clay's shoulders are so broad and blocky it looks like he's put his suit jacket on without first removing it from some giant hanger.

"Workin' for the Man, Clay, same's always."

"Hey man, try not to sound so revved up! No, seriously, do I hear you're in some kind of rut over there with Lon? He trying to pound you in a square hole, is he? Nothing you and me need to talk about, is it?" conjuring with the palms.

"Naw, I'm jake. Thanks." Just love my compassionate coworkers and their not-so-hidden agendas. Clay tells me I'd make a damn fine sales rep, a damn fine one. I'm flattered I guess, but like you'd expect from his title, he's an accomplished hustler. Which is to say I don't agree, I think to make a damn fine sales rep, you have to be one of those fearless old football heroes

Fig. III.10

Tap water filtration system's ill-conceived mascot "Frothy" appears as decal on filtration units.

we see sheepdogging clients through the office on tour. People
used to having things go their way, with commanding voices and
that invincible, athletic carriage, upbeat, indomitable, rehearsed,
lots of things that I'm not. But you tell that to Clay.

Who's busy describing himself as a "hard man to deny," and
going on about the trappings of his success, things I might have
for myself if I became a 'closer' in his 'squad.' He consults his
Rolex 3 or 4 times in our 5-minute conversation to drive the point.
He mentions the boat he sails on weekends, how he's really into
that, how I've probably noticed some nautical leanings in his
'look,' canvas belts and double-breasted jackets and tie-tacks of
tiny sloops and seagulls. Sure, I have no problem picturing him on
his boat: "Hey put that down. Don't touch that. You don't know what
you're doing. Keep doing that if you want to lose an arm, mister."

That's how he runs his team too, like he's ordering them around
on his boat, only they're not the crew of gung-ho bastards he'd like
to think. He's got one of the worst turnover problems in the company. Hence his interest in my transfer, I think. Not because I'm
looking burnt or because I'd make a damn fine sales rep but because
I'd help him manufacture the image of sales as a place where everyone
wants in, rather than out.

"...and haven't I been on some dynamite vacations," Clay sez
dreamily, rounding third on his recruiting bid. He makes a final display of the watch, wobbling his wrist until it peeks out from his
cuff. "Tell you what, Thornton, it's one hell of a ride, our team." I
tell him it certainly sounds that way, and that when things get ugly
in CS I'll hunt him down for sure. That winsome smile shows a trace
of effort.

"Good enough. Don't wait too long, now. You know right where I'll
be?" Yes, I do. He sends me off with such a macho clout on the back
that my first couple steps are involuntary.

You have got to know what it is you want, or someone is going to sell you a bill of goods along the
line that can do irreparable damage to your self-esteem....

REF. NO. 68) *See notes, pp. 148-151*   AUTHOR(S)   **Richard Nelson Bolles**

Here's a chestnut from the good ol' days of plant labor, a favorite
story of my grandfather's. The setting's an old Westinghouse factory now
lying empty in the suburbs, or specifically it's a men's room in that
factory. A dozen men are packed in there, smoking cigarettes and shouting at each other (they're all wearing earplugs). Outside, over a racket
of machinery, you can hear orchestral variations on 'Somewhere a Hill.'
The flip side is 'Sugar Blues' and this is the only 45 in the place,
spun all day side to side. As more men steal into the room, cigarette
smoke plumes out, hangs beside the door for a moment and dissolves.

Presently a squat older man comes into view, straining with a red 2-
wheel dolly on which he's propped a vented metal box. Extending from the
machine, which is a refrigeration unit, is a black rubber hose whose
free end he's got clamped in his fist. He boots the door open and hauls
the machine inside. Conversation stops short. The door closes behind him
and save for the machines and 'Somewhere a Hill,' all's quiet.

Then FWOOM! The door's flung open again and out spill all the men in
coveralls, charging through a gout of white vapor. Shouts of "Holy mack-
erel!" and "What's the big idea?" and other War-era expressions of alarm
are heard. The older man's the last one to emerge, red-faced and breathing into the back of his wrist. "There's ya cigarette break ya bastards!" he's wheezing. "There's ya cigarette break!" He flaps his free
hand around in the cloud of Freon he's loosed on his workers. Bootheels
decrescendo across the assembly floor. "Ya wort'less, ya wort'less, sonsabitches!" He pauses for a minute, and tosses on a few more expletives
in the way you might tamp out a mostly empty catsup bottle.

Then he yells "Murphy!" and waddles up to another man, who's wearing a
short-sleeved white oxford like his own. He comes to within an arm's
length of my (distaff) grandfather and says quietly but with great feeling: "I'm stuck here. You're gonna be stuck here too (my grandfather
stayed for exactly three and a half more hours, as it turned out). This,
I have no problem wit' being stuck here. You'll learn, you're gonna learn
what it's like, and I won't tell you nothing good or bad about it except
what it is. But there is one thing I'm asking for, while I'm here, and
this you should know, it's the only goddamned thing I want. I want to sit
up in that cage, I want to look down
on all them working the floor, and I
want to say: 'look at those sonsabitches go.' That's it. I wanna be able to
look down on them like a kid wit' a
ant farm, and I want to say 'look at
those sonsabitches go.'"

3:40 PM -- Alert the Media: Thornton Catches a Break

Mid-afternoon doldrums have set in, Clay not being a huge help in this regard. My coffee mug isn't twenty minutes dry and already I'm cycling low again. I stand up to stretch after a few calls, land heavily in my chair again and bring up a Web browser on my PC. An internal line goes off.

"Thornton? Rebby Conlon. Got a second?"

Rebby Conlon, Creative Director of the design group. Gretchen the temp, this morning, on Rebby Conlon: *Oh gawd, Rebby Conlon is one of the gawds of design, you just, I mean that brain ends up in a jar at a museum, do you understand me? You just don't know how talented, oh and nice? Rebby's so nice....*

"Mm-hmmh, of course. What's going on?"

"Just got out of a status meeting with John McKenna and he mentioned you might be interested in some kind of discussion with me, some kind of...graphic designer-y discussion maybe?"

"Absolutely. Yeah, I'd just, I wanted to talk with someone up there, nothing that has to happen right away. I'm thinking not so much in terms of graphic design as, more along the lines of photography? I'm going to have more questions than anything else...."

"Good, that's probably a good place to start. So listen, I don't know what you're up to right now, but my 3:45 canceled on me. If you can spare a couple minutes would you want to come up...? Ees good, ah?"

Okay. Making my way upstairs now, up to the tenth floor and out to the far end of the building's east wing. This is where they've had the design group put down stakes, past a long hallway of unoccupied offices, out there like some foreign legion garrison. Plenty of time between here and there to draft up the right list of questions for Rebby. You'd think. Truth is, the closer I get to that office the less distinctly I recall what I'm supposed to do there (not feeling the kind of panic, naturally, that would activate the brain). By the time I'm seated before her, I expect I'll have gone fully catatonic. Well. I'm told the informational interviewee expects, will even encourage, a candid display of ignorance from the interviewer. Appears I'll have a chance to test that theory.

If your mind is empty, it is always ready for anything; it is open to everything. In the beginner's mind there are many possibilities; in the expert's mind there are few.

REF. NO. 69)   *See notes, pp. 148-151*   **AUTHOR(S)**   **Shunryu Suzuki**

The studio floor has a couple different levels and is mostly open form, with a lot of space in the center, the walls lined with desks and drafting tables, printer and server stations, all beneath a dou-ble-row of skylights left over from the building's days as a ware-house. Darting through here go a manic and preoccupied bunch of for-matters, junior and senior level designers and art directors, an account service staff, comp illustrators and freelance photographers, micro sales and production staffs and some sleep-deprived looking new media people. It's goatee <u>madness</u> up here, and the same goes for metallic nail polish and Caesar haircuts, lotsa mean-looking black boots, linen clothing everywhere, pruned and billowy like crepe. Don't mind me, you people, just came here to see Rebby, yes, thank you.

Rebecca Conlon stands about six feet tall, so it's no small relief to find her seated in her office. She's hunched over a legal pad writing feverishly, nor will she pause but only make some vague hand gesture at me when I knock on her door jamb (no doors in here, you see). On her desk the computer is significantly absent. She winds up her writing with a flourish, and adds a period with enough might to have stood her pen on its point. She looks up only when I'm seated opposite her.

Fig. III.11 (a) and (b)

My coffee mug and the rodeo cowboy it's got on it. Never leaves my cube, I bring coffee to it in paper cups and when it's empty I just wipe it out with whatev-er's near to hand, shirt tail, laser paper, etc.

Rebby's got shoulder-length hair, straight and flawless platinum-white with a very retro That Girl flair around the bottom. She's fair-skinned nearly to the point of translucence, enough to give her that road-map look on the eyelids. In fact, I'd think her an albino if it weren't for the eyes themselves, which are a deep

109

Fig. III.12
Brutal-looking rat
trap in Rebby's
office, plunder of
recent photo
shoot. They've
been conducting
experiments in
here, seeing how
different items
stand up to it.
Had one trial with
a felt-tip pen
where the upshot
was, predictably,
dark blue ink
everywhere. Stains
still on Rebby's
desk and phone,
some on the wall
and carpet too.

opalescent blue like you might see on a bowling ball. She's no definite age but I'd guess early forties, possibly mid. And I would think she'd have one or two violent allergies, to something like shellfish, for instance.

"Welcome in, Thornton, nice to put a face to the name and so on. How are they treating you in customer service? How's Lon? I guess if you two were hitting it off you wouldn't be here, right? Hell on earth, then, is that more like it? Don't worry, I won't keep answering my own questions."

Not sure if it's my turn to talk, but I do and I get right to it. I tell her what I told McKenna, that I feel as though I'm being punished for something. She suggests evil doings in a past life and I comment that I must have been one top-flight bastard.

"Well you're forgiven. Look, I've got a conference call in 20 minutes so we won't get too far today. But I wanted you to come up and get comfortable poking around. To hear John tell it, you're in some distress."

"Well, I may've overstated my case, of course, I do that."

"Sure well here you are. Why don't we start, actually where did you go to school?"--as though the question's been nagging her--"Tell me...what you studied in college."

"College? I'm afraid I was making the whole liberal arts scene, it had nothing to do with any of this, really."

"Oh me neither, I was convinced I was going to be a journalist so I majored in English, go figure. Nothing to be ashamed of, Thornton, half our staff kind of backed into this, ahh, the 'biz.' We found Abby working in a Perfumania at the Three Corners Galleria."

"Okay, well, I was never too interested in my major, like to the point where I stopped showing for classes. Those colise-

um-size lectures we had? Forget about it, I'd skip those
altogether. The smaller ones, the discussion sections where
I'd have been missed, I made them as a rule. But I wasn't
doing any of the reading, I'd be in there just freestyling
my ass off. Which I guess was an education in itself." Can't
say why I'd be volunteering this.

"So you decided, what? there was nothing in college worth
learning?"

"In political science? No, I wasn't considering a career
in government, I learned that much as a freshman."

Rebby saws a forefinger across her chin. "There's a point,
you know, where you'd have to ask yourself what you're doing
there in the first place, in college. Like what did you think
the payoff was going to be? What kind of penalty did you imagine there'd be for trying something else?"

"Why didn't I just hang it up, halfway through?"

"Sure, or take some time off. Beats wasting your time in
a situation like that when it's just, obviously gone bankrupt for you. Jump a freighter and go work in the Ivory
Coast, I don't know. That derring-do concept isn't doing
much business today, looks like."

No, and in the tradition of the young malcontent, I blame
society. Really, though, everyone's so obsessed with
advancement and accreditation now that it's hard to make
time for those old-fashioned acts of bravura. Credentials of
one kind or another are tirelessly sought and gained and
merchandised, everyone measuring their own against everyone
else's and gaining from that comparison an idea of self-
worth. We believe the college-aged individual, for instance,

Re: society's obsession with advancement/accreditation: see Abraham Maslow on p. 83.

When we unconsciously drift through life, we cultivate self-doubt, apathy, passivity, and poor judgment. By struggling, by facing the difficulties of making conscious choices, we grow stronger, more
capable, and more responsible to ourselves. Once we see and accept that our talents are also our
blueprint for a satisfying vocational life, then we can stop looking to others for approval and direction.
Choosing consciously also forces us to stop postponing a commitment. In this way we move one step
closer to being responsible, contributing adults.

REF. NO. 70) *See notes, pp. 148-151*   AUTHOR(S)   **Marsha Sinetar**

Most liberal arts graduates do not earn their living in a manner directly connected to their major....The reason why the four-year liberal arts tradition has displayed greater lifelong utility is that the courses offered in four-year programs are not narrowly utilitarian and stress skills of reasoning and inquiry that emerge from an encounter with discrete fields of study. Unfortunately, it is in the arena of undergraduate education that the sameness and uniformity in institutional practice have become damaging and have prevented the finest ideals of a college education from being realized.

The plain fact is that too much is being made out of getting into college and too little about what happens to individuals once there, or about what it takes to graduate from college....[T]he level of general intellectual aspiration and idealism nurtured during college is far too low for comfort.

In their ideal form, the undergraduate years of college ought to be the time when an individual, as an adult, links learning to life....Parents and students often harbor the exclusive illusion that college, in contrast to high school, is about preparing oneself for the practical business of life, a phrase that is often reduced to the earning of money. Too many educators overreact to this legitimate utilitarian claim by preaching about learning for its own sake.

The key to this problem rests in the definition of utility. It turns out that when it comes to education, virtue is its own reward. Learning for its own sake is the best preparation for functioning competitively and creatively....The utility of serious learning and thinking rests most often in its unforeseen consequences.

REF. NO. 71) *See notes, pp. 148-151*   AUTHOR(S)   **Leon Botstein**

ought to be in college and ought to emerge with at least a bachelor's degree. And consciously or not, that's why I stuck it out: college was where the diplomas were dispensed, and I was convinced I needed one; to deviate from that course was to risk consequences uncertain (though certainly disastrous). It's like the old 19th century dilemma of being stuck in a bad marriage for fear of the community's, or the church's, whoever's, censure. Maybe 20 years from now, as mores continue to evolve, we'll have as many kids leaving college as we've got adults cashing out of wedlock.

...None of which will occur to me until later, of course. For now, I'm telling Rebby it was the classes outside my major that kept me in school.

"Okay good, we ought to concentrate on that," she's saying. "What specifically did you get involved in, in your studio classes?"

"Well, some composition and mechanical basics for starters,

lots of darkroom training, the wet and dry routines, developing and print-making--"

"Mostly black and white--"

"--primarily, yeah, but I've done Cyanotype and Argyrotype prints too."

"And...you weren't just working with your point and shoot?"

"Oh, no, I borrowed all kinds of equipment, from friends or from the department. I worked with this one instructor's Hasselblad a lot, which is of course what I'm trying to buy now, like a used 500C or CM. I even used some old vintage rigs, though I don't remember what the point of that was."

"But you have samples of your classroom work?"

"Oh yes, a shoebox full of prints, some in a binder, some 2 1/4's and a handful of slides. A few pieces were run in student publications and a couple in our campus daily. I got real into it, which of course led to speculation about some kind of career in photography, not like I knew where to begin."

"Well this is where you'll begin, actually."

"Um, great." Ignorance, and the candid display thereof.

"And the next step is your book. Have you given any thought to that? To showcasing your best

Time Killer Grab-bag

Coffee (employee facility): 5 min.
 —percolator running low: add 5 min.

Coffee (external): 15 min.

Water: 5 min.

Phone call to friends (lim. 6/day); friend is:
—employed, enjoying it: 5-10 min.
—employed, disillusioned: 15-20 min.
—unemployed: 20-30 min.

Copy/fax: 5 min.

Check printer: 5 min.
—appear to check/reload toner: add 5 min.

Something's come up/emergency errand/ brazen walk-out: 30 min.

En-route conversation with coworker: add 15 min. to any of the above

work in some kind of portfolio or slide set, something
you could tote around?"

"I--sure--but I haven't got enough material yet, not
of the caliber--"

"No no, you only need 6 or 7 good shots, even a
couple of pieces will get people talking if they're
flash enough, the pictures I mean. Think of your average art director's attention span, right? You'll have 5
minutes, tops. And then think about how you'd play your
work to these people, in that time window. And of
course you can't ever stop running around with your
camera now and shooting, whatever, anything, just taking more pictures. Lots and lots of them. Just never
put your rig down, wear it on your neck, go nuts."

"Oh yeah, I'm doing that already, you know, as time
and money permit...."

"And we can say you're not all that interested in
layout or production?"

"No, I mean sure, I could do something like that, I
was doing paste-up for a few student publications,
fine-art type quarterlies, and after junior year I did
some desktop work. And I'm up with most of the current
software now too, just with my job being what it is."

"But that isn't the way you'd prefer to go, is it?
Listen, you don't want to land anywhere by default,
least of all in design. You wouldn't be any happier
there than in CS. Don't get beguiled by the whole
'creative industry' bit (fluttering her hands around
like a sorceress). There are a million jobs in the
applied arts that would send you back to Lon grateful,
difficult as that is to believe right now. Okay? So
did you just like shooting the pictures, or did you
get into printing them too, that whole darkroom-mole
routine?"

"Both, I liked both ends of it, actually."

"Good, because here's one thing, if you're interested, you can get some dynamite experience as a darkroom technician. Though you should know, any job on
those lines is going to pay a starvation wage, assuming you get one in the first place. But what you do

is work some other part-time job at the same time, and
you could volunteer any other time you have--actually you
could do this now--you could assist some local artist on
shoots or in the lab. When you're ready to carve out some
time, I'll give you a list of shooters who use free help-
-which could turn into a paid position. But again it
depends on what you consider being paid. There's that, oh
and have you ever thought about photo-research?"

"Not really, actually I don't think I'm sure what
that...is."

"Photo-researchers look through stock catalogues and
in-house collections and help designers pick out their
shots. You spend a lot of time deciphering photo specs
and dickering with stock houses, but you end up contract-
ing a lot of shoots too, so there's your networking
opportunity. I'll have Mark, our Mark, send you down some
stock books and you can get the drift. I'm sure you could
hit him up for a lunch appointment. He'd have more to
tell you about photo-research than I would."

"That sounds...that's great."

"What else. Please come around here whenever you'd
like. We're always ass-over-elbows but you can look
through our library, ask questions, people here are fine
with that, they only dress like rock stars. They're really, genuinely, affable people. Talk to them and call me.
I can certainly help critique your book, and we can work
on your presentation--very important. So. Sorry we don't
have more time to dig into this...."

"No, are you kidding? I can't tell you how much you've
helped already, I mean this just pushed me as far forward
in 20 minutes as I would have done in another year downstairs."

"Good, well make sure you keep at it. I can't tell you
how many people back out of here and I never hear from
them again. I don't get many repeat visits from you young
waywards, seems to me."

"No way. I'll be back with something to show you, soon
I hope. So okay thanks, thanks a lot. I don't need to
take up any more of your time. Thank you."

Consider the following writings (again with the 'GenX' caveat). The idea here is that the angst-ridden youth is a figure that resurfaces throughout the ages, having always much in common with its previous and future avatars (cv. pp. 97-8); at the same time, though, many of the troubled youth's anxieties will have generation-specific roots:

Much of the uncertainty experienced by Xers as they grew up, though, came from the generational debris Boomers left in their wake. Forget what the idealistic Boomers intended, Xers say, and look instead at what they actually did: Divorce. Latchkey kids. Homelessness. Soaring national debt. Bankrupt Social Security. Holes in the ozone layer. Crack. Downsizing and layoffs. Urban deterioration. Gangs.... Boomers overindulged, heedless of the consequences, bequeathing a world in tatters, a world with difficult, uncertain prospects for the future.

REF. NO. 72) *See notes, pp. 148-151*   AUTHOR(S) **Yankelovich Partners, Inc.**

. . . .

Divorce is deceptive. Legally it is a single event, but psychologically it is a chain—sometimes a never-ending chain—of events, relocations, and radically shifting relationships strung through time, a process that forever changes the lives of the people involved.

REF. NO. 73) *See notes, pp. 148-151*   AUTHOR(S)   **Judith Wallerstein**

. . . .

Vigilance and adaptability are important. Since nothing lasts, and is certainly never unfailingly good, you must have the flexibility to change course or have backup plans. You need insurance against the bad consequences that always seem to happen. You must learn to hedge, know how to anticipate, know what to do, and be prepared to move fast.

REF. NO. 74) *See notes, pp. 148-151*   AUTHOR(S) **Yankelovich Partners, Inc.**

. . . .

[T]hough life after divorce may present a rich and stimulating set of new experiences and challenges for adults, it does not have the same impact on children. Children are conservative creatures. They like things to stay the same. Troublingly, divorce makes change the only sure thing in children's family lives.

REF. NO. 75) AUTHOR(S)   **Barbara DaFoe Whitehead**

Xers have had sparse opportunities to witness or experience enduring affiliations of any kind—social, geographical, religious or political. Our own family structures, and those of our peers, have not been reliable. We are unlikely to have spent our childhoods in one community—and even if we did, our childhoods were marked by the characteristics of suburban diaspora and the evisceration of community centers. For these reasons, even our friendship circles have always been in flux, shifting along with forces beyond our control.

[N]othing in Xers' life experience has remained the same long enough to inspire our unquestioning belief. What we believe in most is change and uncertainty.... Xers are looking to ourselves as we always have.... our own resourcefulness, and our comfort with new technologies, remain our most reliable allies for coping in an uncertain world.

REF. NO. 76) *See notes, pp. 148-151*   AUTHOR(S)   **Bruce Tulgan**

. . . .

Xers are determined to be involved, to be responsible, to be in control—and to stop being victimized by life's uncertainties.

They're far better at living with uncertainty than Boomers. The Boomer focus on "live for today" was predicated on their certainty about the limitless future. Boomers were sure the future would take care of itself—that there always would be plenty more, so live for today. Xers are focused on living for today, too, but not because they feel assured about the future, but rather because they can't count on it.

REF. NO. 77) *See notes, pp. 148-151*   AUTHOR(S) **Yankelovich Partners, Inc.**

. . . .

The logic of expressive divorce also suggested that relationships themselves—especially relationships that are binding or permanent—are risky investments. The most reliable form of investment thus becomes the investment in the self. The logic of expressive divorce argued not only for building one's own psychological capital, therefore, but also for keeping it "liquid." A self not tied down by permanent bonds and obligations was a self that could take advantage of new opportunities as they came along.

REF. NO. 78)   AUTHOR(S)   **Barbara DaFoe Whitehead**

Divorce culture, intergenerational legacies and strain, the end of the corporate era: all relate back to the temp lifestyle writings on p. 40 — thankfully your generation seems to thrive on this chain of uncertainties!

"Say...Mark, you look--how do I want to say
this--like no more black squiggle over your
head? Do you mean to tell us you're having a...a
good day?"

Fig. III.13

"Black squiggle,"
used in cartoons
to signify
vexation

   "A good day, no. But the last 25 minutes
have been, well sure, good. I might get a full
half hour in today, like 30 solid minutes of
good."

   "Don't go then, keep me company. You can help
alphabetize or color-code--don't, I know you
like to do both but you'll have to pick just
one...."

   This is Carrie Serabian, who's brand new to
imagesetting as I'm writing, though I imagine
she'll be gone by the time anyone reads this. She's been brought on
to assist John Vespasian, not because he really needed an assistant
or knew how to manage one, but because Senior Management needed to
'move him up' without changing his job description. So they physically moved him to a cube with walls that are only four feet high,
essentially putting him on display, and they gave him a supervisee.

   In his 6 years in imagesetting, John's made himself pretty indis-
pensible, to management certainly but more to his own staff, in a
kind of John Henry, icon-of-the-proletariat way. Anyone in production
will vouch for 'that sumbitch's broad back' where I'm told, paren-
thetically, you'd find a near-actual-sized tattoo of the Temple of
Solomon. He's dedicated, reliable, honest, thrifty, decent, and in no
way prepared for a personal assistant.

   He was spelling it out for me at the summer outing, after I'd
asked him where Carrie was and he'd said Now what's that supposed to
mean. Thought he was just heading off another Serabian/Vespasian quip.
I hadn't realized just how strained the relationship had grown:

   "That whole first week she's there, you know, right on my shoulder,
and I don't have a goddamned thing to give her to do. Christ. Even now
she's got her own desk, but I have to think about it every minute,
what can she do, what can she do. I'm not going to send her to the
mail room or make her do copying or faxing, dictation and that. I mean
you know where she went to school, I ought to be the one taking dictation, am I right? This is why it's an unworkable situation, Mark. I
can't give her my work because if I'm on the line for a job, I'm going
to do it myself, you know what I'm saying? I feel so guilty it's hard
to talk straight to her, even though we get along great. If she wasn't

just a terrific person, which she is, I'd have let her go that first
week, sorry kid, or else tried pushing her off on someone else, it's
just, god-damn. I never asked for an assistant."

So Carrie sits at this quiet little station just off the production floor and e-mails her college friends all day. Her accessibility
and knack for conversation make her desk a kind of oasis for the
bored and shiftless and despondent. Like I say, she's brand new,
still has that Oh Golly look going. I like that. I'm about 6 months
past Oh Golly, but I haven't reached the point where I need to root
it out of the others who still have it. The problem for Carrie is,
there's no lack of people around here who do think that way. If
they're not feeding off that positive energy of hers, they seem to
want to snuff it out.

I saw Tom Ackert, this hard-bitten old guy from shipping, lay
into her on Friday for some overnight delivery snafu she'd played a
bit part in. He informed her that this wasn't college, honey, and
that a late parcel wasn't like a late term paper, that accounts are
won and lost over nickel-and-dime fumbles like this. Told her to
"wake up," with this dyspeptic grin he probably thought was charming. She gave him some kind of glib and good-natured response, yes
she'd certainly be keeping that in mind, which wasn't at all what
Ackert wanted. His smile fell away and he leaned in with his palms
on her counter, it creaking under his weight, and started in, *sotto
voce*, with "now I'm not here to hurt your feelings Carrie. But,
ah...what the hell is wrong with you?" and so forth until he'd truly
upset her, and only then could he leave, satisfied he'd given her a
"long-overdue wakeup call," one she was better off getting from him
than from Senior Management.

What it really is, is that guys like Ackert can't let her get
away with that guileless good cheer of hers. They just love the Ivy-
league-grad-with-no-common-sense routine. As in, if she's so smart,
why doesn't she know to keep a copy of her packing slips; as in,
this may have passed for brains in college but this is work now and
she'd better figure out how unhappy she is if she plans on staying.
Experience, she'll do well to learn, is the antidote to the positive
attitude. Nor does it have to be your own experience, we've got
plenty of old cranks willing to donate theirs, anything to help
break in the happy ingenue. Guys like Ackert may even have been
gung-ho here once but no longer, and when their own glow has faded
they need to stamp it out of others as well, rather like being poi-
son in the final stages of croquet.

So who knows how much longer Carrie will stick it out here.
Can't imagine why she'd want to stay.

Re: the prepared-
ness of
managers,
and the
dubious
rewards of
promotion,
refer back
to pp. 68, 74.

119

4:35 PM -- Happy Trails

Back at my desk now, and just in time to see that patch of sun set and vanish over the little horizon of my workstation wall. Rebby Conlon interview or no, I'm strapping m'self back down to the CS train tracks. On the down side of the caffeine boot too, time to really watch that clock good. The phone starts ringing. Outside they're keeping at it with the jackhammers, which is nice, tearing up the roads to have at some sewer main. There's your metaphor. In my corner of the Land of Opportunity not only are the streets not paved with gold, they're not even paved with paving. "Hello, this is Mark...?" Just a gouged-up moonscape down there, noisy and treacherous and crumbling over god-knows-what below. "What, okay, I'm look-ing that up right now, and--yes but could you please slow down and repeat that please, no we can rerun those and still make the overnight cutoff--sure, right up to 9:15 we can cab it out to the airport so--well yes of course you're upset...."

There is no man, however wise, who has not at some period of his youth said things, or even lived in a way which was so unpleasant to him in later life that he would gladly, if he could, expunge it from his memory. But he shouldn't regret this entirely, because he cannot be certain that he has indeed become a wise man—so far as any of us can be wise—unless he has passed through all the fatuous or unwholesome incarnations by which that ultimate stage must be reached. I know there are young people...whose teachers have instilled in them a nobility of mind and moral refinement from the very beginning of their schooldays. They perhaps have nothing to retract when they look back upon their lives; they can, if they choose, publish a signed account of everything they have ever said or done; but they are poor creatures, feeble descendants of doctrinaires, and their wisdom is negative and sterile. We cannot be taught wisdom, we have to discover it for ourselves by a journey which no one can undertake for us, an effort which no one can spare us.

REF. NO. 79) *See notes, pp. 148-151* AUTHOR(S) **Marcel Proust**

IV

· · · · · · ·

Jay Gathers' Travelling
F.Q.M Dumb Show

—from an article in Forbes entitled 'Loony-Tunes Management Training.'

They all file in after Jay Gathers like good ducklings, do Senior and middle management. Still snickering over a bit of mirth they've shared in private, some joke to which we, already assembled here and waiting, aren't privy. Tucked militarily beneath every right arm is a new set of TQM marching orders, bound in a glossy black pocket folder with our logo foil-stamped on the front and back covers. Here comes a group equipped to Manage Quality more Totally than ever before.

Anyone who's bought the hoax to this point, that TQM is here to deconstruct our employee-management barriers, need only take note of the seating plan. About ten yards out from the back wall there's a podium and beside it a wheeled booth of some sort draped in olive cloth. Behind these are the black leather chairs of management, describing an arc two rows deep. On the other side of the booth and the podium there's a grid of metal fold-down chairs, 25 seats across and 15 rows deep, welded into a single construction like stadium bleachers (and about as comfortable), intended, need we say, for the rank-and-file. Thus are the have-nots faced squarely into the haves, each side encouraged to contemplate the other and to appreciate the distance between. Managers take their seats and fall to discussing ways in which the worker might be cadged, led, bribed, tricked or strong-armed into TQM, just as we discuss how the system might be dismantled and its captains usurped—or so I imagine. Anyhow, the whole us-and-them thing is seldom in greater evidence.

This is one of those meetings that's compulsory in every respect but in name. I'd say 9 of us in 10 are here, most with pens poised over steno pads as tech guys test the P.A. and cart in one of those ubiquitous flipcharts. CS is all accounted for except for Pitcher, who

has opted out, very likely at Lon's
behest. We in CS share the feeling that
Jason's days among us are numbered.

Find I've written "TQM 7/19 aft mtg."
My notebooks are full of hopeful lead-
ins like this, with nothing but bad
sketches and drafts of personal letters
to separate them. I think I put the
headings there on the off chance that
we'll learn something of substance in
one of these meetings.

No sooner is his flipchart in place,
though, than Gathers is writing 'TEAM-
WORK' vertically down the left margin, a
word he'll no doubt have to work into
some happy acronym. I decide I've had quite enough TQM for today, and
that no one's going to notice the headphone wires reaching from my collar to the tiny speakers tucked in my ears. So with Jay's undercard,
our President herself, taking the podium to listless applause, I've got
Nat Hayward spinning the monster hits of the 1970's and early '80's for
my lo-ong commute home.

In this way the presentation takes on the appearance of mime, like
an old-fashioned dumb show. A crooked smile from our President means
she's leading in with some workplace drollery (I imagine that she reads
the words "pause for laughter" from her notes by mistake). She waits
for much unctuous laughter to subside, shows us the crown of her head,
working her mouth like a landed fish, gestures stiffly to a beaming
Jay Gathers, offers him a handshake and cedes the podium. Our man
swaggers up with fists propped on his belt, looking like nothing so
much as a school superintendent or corrections officer from the early
1960's. A full Amish-style beard without a moustache is showing signs
of grizzle, he's lanky and tough-looking, spry with a mix of intelligence and menace in a dangerously attentive pair of eyes--which he's
part-way hidden behind a pair of photogreys that make Steve Schimmer's
machine shop goggles seem haute by comparison.

Fortunately for the dumb show, Gathers has lugged in a huge inventory of props. There's a great double fan-blade tagged 'winds of
change,' a length of chain styled 'our team,' and a mini see-saw that
he adjusts on its fulcrum until--voilà--it achieves balance. Through
the headphones I can hear the audience's laughter, rising in discreet
little pockets at first, begin to grow general. The initials on the
flipchart yield: Together Everyone Acts More Willing, Organized,
Resourceful and Kreative.

Fig. IV.1

Parents: which of these men
would you sooner have watching over your children?

1. Clean-
shaven,
no glasses

2. Amish
beard,
photogreys

But the presentation doesn't really take off until it's 45 minutes old, and he sweeps the curtain from that mysterious booth. Which turns out to be a three-paneled plexiglass enclosure, the opening faced toward management, with a single shelf at about waist-height, and on it an upright length of black rubber tubing 6 inches high and almost as many wide, like a section of stovepipe. Gathers' hands disappear behind the podium and reemerge cupping a bowling-ball-sized melon.

A great commotion rises over the accounting group as Karen Fendi stands and approaches him. After some interaction with her staff in the audience she writes 'Procrastination' across the melon and holds it aloft to general applause. She then sets it on the rubber mount in the booth.

From this point the meeting devolves into a Gallagher-esque stage show, complete with drop-cloths for the floor and raingear for everyone behind the podium. Managers write their groups' most damaging flaws on a series of melons and select, from a barrel of sledgehammers, the one they'll use to pound (figuratively, at least) their professional demons apart in the booth. It's brilliant. Down go tardiness, poor communication, inattention to detail, boredom, inefficiency, politics, time-hoarding and prima donna-ism. The mess on the stage is incredible. I'll give Gathers credit for this, at least, my headphones are off and I'm going as spastic as anyone.

Lon's performance here is worth noting. Having inscribed
his melon with 'Apathy,' Lon takes too big a sledgehammer
and deals the melon a glancing blow, sends it ricocheting
off the side of the booth and across the stage. Off it
rolls, Lon giving chase in his rain slicker, only too aware
of the symbolism in this. "Get it Lon!" we're all scream-
ing. He wrangles it back to the mount and, with a smaller
hammer this time, and with the head turned sideways, flat-
tens his melon successfully. But he's not finished: he
gathers fallen pieces of rind from the floor and pulverizes
them too, and takes a few extra swings at whatever's left
on the shelf, pieces of his melon and everyone else's. He's
just going bananas, and the managers behind him exchange
looks of concern. We're all starting to think he might have
to be dragged off, when he stops, his face crimson and fit
to burst, his chest heaving massively, and he finds the
strength to raise the hammer, two-fisted, over his head.
That just about brings the house down. I don't remember
ever having laughed so hard at work.

(Later in a private session, Gathers talks the incident
through with Lon: "You tried what you saw everyone else
doing and with your problem, for your team, it didn't work.
Then what did you do? You came at it again with a different
solution, you turned your mallet-head lengthwise, and the
problem vanished ..." Lon nodding along gravely.)

Anyhow, melon-nacht ends with all three owners of the
company going tandem on a watermelon labeled 'TQM Foot-
Dragging.' They smash it up pretty good. When we stand to
applaud Gathers at the end of his presentation, I'm right
there on my feet with all the rest--which I never would
have believed at 11 this morning. But hell, I mean, they
were up there smashing melons, for the love o' god.

                    *   *   *

There are some second-shift imagesetters on cigarette
break in the employee lounge and that's where I am now,
watching the first shift come gamboling back from the big
meeting. There's much boisterous talk in the hallway, bodies caroming playfully off each other. "Suckers," sez a guy
named Kahlil, and there's some harsh laughter, like hiss-

ing, people venting smoke through their teeth. Glad these guys didn't see me five minutes ago, hopping around with the rest of CS, all of us whomping each other on the back like a bunch of apes. Glad too they don't know what I'm waiting here for, which would be a private audience with our Dr. Gathers.

Not that I could say why, precisely. I've just been meaning to corner him, since this morning or even earlier on, for some of the same reasons that I'm keeping this journal. I'd like to explain my situation to him or at least take a stab, see what kind of wisdom he might bring to bear from a career's worth of occupational consulting. Not like we'd have been busting those melons at the behest of a wise man, necessarily, but I've got to think he'd have some experience with questions like mine, that I could cull something useful from a one-on-one with him. Either that or this really is the act of desperation I suspect it to be.

In any case, I wait until the long parade of yahoos (of whom I have to say I was one) tapers off. When it does I snuff my cigarette, excuse myself and slink back to the conference area. Here a special detachment of the building crew is breaking the stage area down, and Jay's addressing a few managers and star employees who've rushed the dais. He's clearly trying to get out of here. He keeps saying "...anyhow" and "...well alright then" but he's not shaking anybody. He registers me with a look you might see on a trussed-up steer. I don't guess I'm helping him much, standing here shifting my weight from one foot to another, holding a section of my lower lip in my teeth, I'm just ten less minutes he'll get with his family tonight.

But I actually help to spring him, as it turns out. He says "...anyhow I've got a train to make. I'll just see what this young gentleman needs and then find my way out. Thank you all for being so great. I think we scored heavily here today, no?" &c. Time for panic to pay me another visit, only it's worse now than waiting to meet Rebby-- can't seem to confront anyone on this subject without my body doing its insurrection bit. My openers flee one at a time and leave nothing behind but static. Old tin taste in

126

the gullet now too, oxygen situation growing tenuous, organs assuming battle stations, blood rushing out in every inconvenient direction. Here he comes, here he comes here he

"Ehm, Mr. Gathers, hi. Just, very quickly please..."

"Very quickly," he chirps.

"You bet. I'm Mark Thornton, CS employee here, customer service." The group behind him falls silent. "I just needed to ask you, I thought I could explain a problem to you and get your reaction. I've been here for 18 months now and what's happening, I'm dealing with this terrible sense of stalemate here, I've got this cribbed-in, kind of restless feeling that's, I feel like it's a fairly common complaint you'd get from my, ehm, generation." Somebody please tell me that's not what I just said. "Idleness, okay? but it's not like I'm an idle person, I don't lack ambition, the problem's the opposite, I feel like I've squandered 18 months here, like I should have been learning a whole different set of skills--"

"Okay, I'll cut in and let you get some air, heh. Let's relax." My breathing's choppy, adrenalated. "I'll tell you

Corporate transitive verbs

— Grow: "Priority one, we all know, is growing the company into the millennium."

— Overnight: "Do you realize that if you overnight those proofs you'll be sending them six blocks across town by way of Memphis Tennessee?"

— Lunch: "Start shuffling my afternoon appointments, will you? I just found out we're lunching those hardballers from Shearson today."

— Office: "You get me a video link and a modem line in here by noon, we're gonna office these guys right from our goddamned hotel room."

— Foreground: "It's just a shame it took a series of layoffs to foreground our file-storage problems."

— Sunset: "You won't be seeing Maxwell in these meetings any more, we've decided to sunset that ridiculous profit-sharing program of his."

this, Matt (Matt?), you're going to be flat-out amazed at the number of new skills and techniques you're going to pick up in the next--"

"Sure, TQM skills, but--"

"Hold on there," Gathers affronted, "you misunderstand. No way, these are <u>life</u> skills, young man. Long after the training, you're going to use these skills to negotiate a life: <u>your</u> life."

"Oh?"

"<u>Oh</u>? Of <u>course</u>. Now. I hear you asking me this: how is TQM going to bring some life back into my job, and bring my job back into my life. Am I right?"

"Uh-huh, yes."

He considers this with his arms akimbo, then one hand jumps to his chin and scrabbles into a thicket of grey hairs there. "Tell you something. I like the way your generation is thinking, Matt. That mantle of the 'slacker' aside. No, what I see is a great deal of ambition, and I see the desire to self-improve. And you, you're a prime example. Okay, but what I also see is a lot of defiance, a great deal of alienation, this, eww I don't know, this <u>restlessness</u>. Sounding familiar?" Familiar because I just said it. "What you may not grasp is that TQM is engineered for getting results, the kind of answers I hear you, and you're not alone either, or even your generation, everyone wants the answer. And all you have to do? It's easy really. Give you a hint: you're already doing it. Don't stop asking the questions, Matt. Of yourself, of your team. Otherwise how do you expect to find any answers? Good enough? Now if you'll excuse me--"

"--Sure but I still haven't heard--"

[L]et me make a general observation—the test of a first-rate intelligence is the ability to hold two opposed ideas in the mind at the same time, and still retain the ability to function. One should, for example, be able to see that things are hopeless and yet be determined to make them otherwise.

REF. NO. 82)   *See notes, pp. 148-151*   AUTHOR(S)   **F. Scott Fitzgerald**

"--Ah-ah, going to stop you right there. I, me, my, mine. Words to edit from your vocabulary. That's yesterday. My problems, my solutions. Pah. Those first-person singulars, they'll kill you. The first person in business is the team, remember I told you that. It's teamwork that gets it done now. Who built the great railroads, Matt: Morgan? Carnegie? Nope. Hundreds of thousands of Chinamen, all working in concert, one big machine we made here with parts shipped in from China. Your generation, though, if there's any direction at all, it's every different way at once. See what I mean? Mobilize your team, and--no, right now we're listening and processing but we're not talking-- get the team going, fire up the customer service team. They'll take you where you want to go. That's the heart of TQM, Matt. Heart and brain and muscles. Think that over and talk to your facilitator. Now I really must go or I'm going to miss my train. I think you people are making some giant quality strides, I told your bosses so. You keep it up and I'll be back."

Jay hitches his briefcase strap up on his shoulder and does a Babe Ruth film-reel routine for all the toadies behind him, sanguine smile and hand-wave, and then a wink and a thumbs-up, all in lightning succession. They can't help but offer him more applause, which he kindly dismisses: "Oh enough, enough you guys."

When he turns to leave, I'm standing there holding my journal up to his face like it's some kind of talisman.

"Mr. Gathers this is a TQM journal I'm using to report on a workday here. I'm writing it today as a matter of fact. Whatever happens to me today I write it down, like our conversation for instance, it's going right in this book. This is a test run for a new program here, and if it helps my performance enough, everyone's going to start keeping these. But it all starts with this one right here," thumping on it with an index finger. "I'm not asking you questions to provoke you, or to flatter you either, but because I really have to know if your program can be made to work for me."

When I withdraw the journal I can see his face

The whole function of philosophy ought to be to find out what definite difference it will make to you and me, at definite instants of our life, if this world-formula or that world-formula be the true one.

William James

129

again, where that avuncular grin is ceding ground to a
more contemplative scowl. We regard each other like this
without speaking for nearly another minute. Then he has me
follow him to the elevator. We leave my managers gaping
after us.

Gathers keeps his eyes rooted to the floor but cuts
them now and then over to my journal, which seems to be
working some weird influence over him so I keep it outside
my bag, like I might even start taking dictation.

"Matt--"

"Mark, actually..."

"Mark, yes. You've caught me with all my materials
packed up in here, Mark," he gives his shoulder bag a
jounce, "which...you see?"

"Well I don't mind keeping it just conversational, no
call for charts and that business. My question is just, I'm
feeling stifled here and undervalued and bored and held
down, and I'm wondering what that's got to do with TQM?"

"Well everything, Mark. That's an easy one, heh."
Gathers fleetingly glib, takes a look at the journal and
clears his throat into his fist. "You know, I should have
you run your questions through my success triads. It's a
TQM diagnostic model. You take a subject, break it down,
come at it again. Give you an example. Interpersonal conflict? Okay, let's go. Break it down: Needs. Values.
Perceptions. Now look at that same conflict again: are
there values that need clarification? What about needs,
are there any needs going unaddressed? That's the power of
the success triad. Questions beget better questions beget
answers. Get it?"

"--"

Jay exhales sharply through his nose. He's vexed but
not, I don't think, at me. "Hmm. There again, the triad's
a fairly advanced TQM technique, and your problem is what
we call 'beginner's mind,' i.e., you have a willingness to
self-improve, but it's undercut by your limited access to
the TQM solution engines. None of this is your fault, but
you can't grasp and enjoy team technology like some of the

more mature officers here (and <u>mature</u> is just a word I'm using for <u>better-trained</u>)."

"Which I accept, but my point is, take a guy who doesn't have any advanced management training--"

"But you're asking an advanced question though, aren't you? To handle it you'd need access to advanced techniques. Think about it. We're talking sustainable behavioral overhaul here, this isn't widgets per hour, or industrial robots."

"Yes, that's precisely the difference. Although first of all if you read my job description and then read one for an industrial robot, you might not know which is which. But, so we've got this new program in place that's going to make me a 'fully realized professional,' right? And all I've seen so far is the props, the charts and the new vocabulary, everyone in management's so keen on the future and these 'teams' that I think they're overlooking the individual..." Gathers waiting for me to trail off. Barely notice our elevator arriving, just note that we're standing in it now. Then we've stepped into the lobby and begun down the long corridor that ends in the employee garage. Which wouldn't be his way out if he'd truly had a train to catch.

"Mark," Gathers explains, after a pause, "I think you need to open your mind a little wider, shake off some of your preconceptions about management systems. I can actually teach you this as a physical exercise, like calisthenics. Push out the reactionary, welcome change (he enacts this as we walk, like a tai-chi move). Looks ridiculous right? Supposed to, it's meant to shake people up, imbalance is one of our keys to unlocking openmindedness. Glasses for the myopic, open your eyes, Matt (his fingers in 'okay' signs over his eyes). Leave your comfort zone just for that one hour in the week, don't worry, you can always go back! Heh. Tell yourself 'today I'll be receptive to something new and unfamiliar....'"

"Fine, but I--"

"Listen, stop for a minute." And here he actually

arrests me with a hand on my cuff. "Listen to yourself. Do you imagine you're the only kid who's lighting out in a career not knowing where you're going, but feeling like anywhere else is better than where you are? Wondering how this fits in with the big cosmic design, with some happy picture of the future you're trying to complete or maintain or re-execute? Did you think at your age that you'd already be a fully realized professional? Do you think anyone else is, at any age? Do you think the overbearing or unresponsive manager just came into being this year, in your neighborhood? Just slow down. You're young and you're not supposed to know what's going on. And don't expect this to change too quickly." His tone is calm, reasonable and, finally, assured.

It's only when he tries to bring it all around to TQM that the spell's broken: "Imagine there are two faces to TQM, okay? There's the technical: charting, tolerances, quotas and what-have-you; and then the human principles: group decision making, process management--the second face. Your job is building the integrative model for Matt Thornton, based on his own unique set of quality beliefs. That's right, do it yourself, I'm not going to do it for you. Surprised?" &c.

(**A hidden lesson in the TQM palaver, though: this is the language he's used to sell himself and his program to Senior Management--the same managers for whom, at some point, I've got a summation brief to write. Hmm. I might actually get something out of this discussion, despite both of our best efforts.... **)

Well done, Dr. Gathers. Refer back to p. 95 for more on setting age-appropriate expectations for yourself (still more readings in this vein coming up).

/32

"No, I'm not surprised, I think I expected to hear something like that."

"Oh, look: if it's a disappointment to you that I haven't spelled out the secrets of the universe for you in 15 minutes, what can I say? I'm a management consultant, this isn't an occupation for philosopher-kings. But I have given you a head start. That's a good primer in high-level TQM you just had, as good as you're going to get in 15 minutes. A-and if you want to record what I've said in that journal, even if it seems like we're not connecting here, you go right ahead. I think I came on a little strong with some high-level terms and techniques, and usually I try and pace myself for beginners. But I tell you what, if you write down exactly what I said, no editorializing I mean, let whoever-else just read that for now. You're going to get some more TQM training and come back to that journal--and remember the questions you have now, because guess what? you'll be looking into a book full of answers."

"Yes of course, I'm just writing this down for now. And, I don't mean to be badgering you, this is just obviously very important to me."

"To me too. Believe it. Hey, why else do you think I'm in this business? It ain't for the money, kid. I help corporations. And I help people, that's what I do. That's why I'll come back here, and I'll remember the session we had today, and so will you, am I right? Well alright. What's your goal then? Zero defects. Got to believe you're gonna make it if you're ever gonna make it. Bye now."

Getting ready to thank him for his time, in earnest, but he just raises a thumb over his head and vanishes down the hall.

It is too clear and so it is hard to see.
A dunce once searched for a fire with
   a lighted lantern.
Had he known what fire was,
He could have cooked his rice much sooner.

Zen commentary

But isn't it incredibly naive to expect life to have a coherent overall meaning? ...It is true that life has no meaning, if by that we mean a supreme goal...that is valid for every individual...it does not follow that life cannot be *given* meaning. But...[i]f a person sets out to achieve a difficult enough goal, from which all other goals logically follow, and if he or she invests all energy in developing skills to reach that goal, then actions and feelings will be in harmony, and the separate parts of life will fit together—and each activity will "make sense" in the present, as well as in view of the past and of the future. In such a way it is possible to give meaning to one's entire life.

REF. NO. 8 4) *See notes, pp. 148-151* AUTHOR(S) **Mihaly Csikszentmihalyi**

. . . .

By the criteria I used, self-actualization does not occur in young people. In our culture at least, youngsters have not yet achieved identity, or autonomy, nor have they had time enough to experience an enduring, loyal, post-romantic love relationship, nor have they generally found their calling, the altar upon which to offer themselves. Nor have they worked out their *own* system of values; nor have they had experience enough (responsibility for others, tragedy, failure, achievement, success) to shed perfectionistic illusions and become realistic; nor have they generally made their peace with death; nor have they learned how to be patient; nor have they learned enough about evil in themselves and others to be compassionate; nor have they had time to become post-ambivalent about parents and elders, power and authority; nor have they generally become knowledgeable and educated enough to open the possibility of becoming wise; nor have they generally acquired enough courage to be unpopular, to be unashamed about being openly virtuous, etc.

REF. NO. 8 5) *See notes, pp. 148-151* AUTHOR(S) **Abraham Maslow**

. . . .

Maybe philosophical problems are hard not because they are divine or irreducible or meaningless or workaday science, but because the mind of *Homo sapiens* lacks the cognitive equipment to solve them. We are organisms, not angels, and our minds are organs, not pipelines to the truth. Our minds evolved by natural selection to solve problems that were life-and-death matters to our ancestors, not to commune with correctness or to answer any question we are capable of asking.

REF. NO. 8 6) *See notes, pp. 148-151* AUTHOR(S) **Steven Pinker**

. . . .

Come now! ...Were everything clear, all would seem to you vain. Your boredom would populate a shadowless universe with an impassive life made up of unleavened souls. But a measure of disquiet is a divine gift. The hope which, in your eyes, shines on a dark threshold does not have its basis in an overly certain world.

REF. NO. 8 7) *See notes, pp. 148-151* AUTHOR(S) **Marcel Proust**

V

. . . .

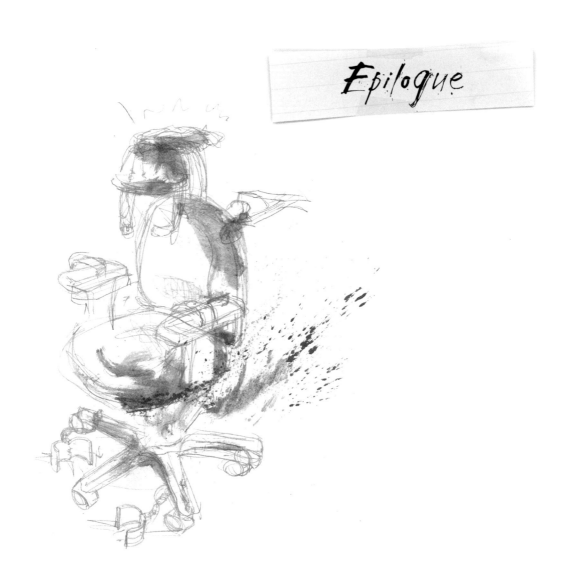

Epilogue

EE: Mark Thornton, THOR/M3996
Date: 02.18
Re: SysCorp IDJ Program/Summation Brief
Title: Inner Destination Journal? More like "Personalized Quality
    Management Toolbox."

The average employee, given his or her limited event horizon and "beginner's mind," may wonder just how soft-side programs like the Journal fit
into a broader quality management commitment:

- How will my Journal translate into a quantifiable improvement of
  my on-the-job performance?

- What kind of results-oriented, "take-charge" measures are built into
  my Journal that will boost my performance indices? and finally:

- How can a program like the IDJ give my on-the-job performance a
  measurable "boost"?

Want to sponsor the Inner Destination Journal (IDJ) company-wide? I'd
brace for an outpouring of challenge-anxiety from known company
change-resisters. But it won't last for long!

Dr. Jason "Jay" Gathers, with whom my IDJ has brought me into ongoing
personal contact, has no lack of dynamic thoughts to share when the subject is implementation strategy. He sees implementation as the catalytic
blending of change initiatives with the pre-existing corporate culture. And
though he's made no specific reference to the Journal *per se*, when he
speaks of the "culturally tuned initiative," the implication is obvious.

And Dr. Gathers maintains that it's the superior management team that
takes this kind of "culturally tuned" approach to continual improvement.
Unorthodoxy needn't trouble the manager with the greatest procedural
longview—in fact, this is precisely the kind of management necessary to

— 1 —

master the challenge of unorthodoxy, to pilot the organization across alien waters (*i.e.*, the Journal) to the far shores of success (*i.e.*, world-class customer satisfaction). Without an eye to the horizon, we light out rudderless.

However, even the most far-sighted management team, Gathers avers, might be wary of a program whose results would seem to resist quantification. Fortunately, this is not the case with the Journal. Soft-side or no, this is a program with "legs." Here are some of the immediate and fairly stunning results of my Journal experience:

SUCCESS TRIADS: SIGNPOSTS OF TQM

The first and most rewarding development has come in the form of the success triad, an advanced situation-mapping technique that TQM beginners like myself are seldom able to apply. But armed with this most powerful tool, I've turned my IDJ into a self-discovery workbook, and effectively "hit one out of the park."

It's almost easy, not to mention fun. The journal foregrounds a series of questions--

- How can I be of the greatest value to myself, my clients, my managers, my corporation?
- How can I identify, isolate, and reproduce performance enhancers, while detouring around setbacks?
- How can I effectively "raise the bar"?

Answers are to be found in two success triads, each of my own devising:

- Life—Career—Success; and
- Internal/external clients—Mark Thornton—Internal/external vendors

With additional thought and effort, I've streamlined Dr. Gathers' model into Success Dyads and Monads.* I've found them equally effective in problem management, and I plan to introduce them to Dr. Gathers himself. I don't imagine I've one-upped him, but I will suggest that even his models should remain open to "continual improvement":

SUCCESS DYADS:

- Challenge—Embrace
- Success—Continuum
- Reversals—There are no reversals

SUCCESS MONADS:

- Success
- Opportunity
- "Race to the Millennium"

KAFKA, EMERSON, SUN TZU—THEY DIDN'T KNOW FROM TQM, RIGHT? THINK AGAIN.

Most of the supplemental writings in my Journal preceded the American advent of TQM by a couple of hundred years, but there's no reason to knock history's great thinkers for being "TQM illiterate." I doubt they'd be surprised to find me reappropriating their wisdom into a TQM value-added commodity, viz. *intellectual capital*. The application paths for the works of Chris Argyris or Marcel Proust might be as numerous and variegated as the sources themselves, but most every SysCorp-supplied writing has had the same result: results.

---

*Like Success Triads, the Dyads and Monads are offered as simple diagnostic models—actual dynamic solutions will have to be achieved on an individual level throughout the corporation. I look forward to further exploration in this area, and to developing even more robust problem-solving engines.

And once more the proof lies in the situation-map pudding. Rather than just list the successes I've enjoyed in the wake of "IDJ-ing it," I've rolled up my sleeves and plotted my quality-management milestones in a fever-chart format, thus:

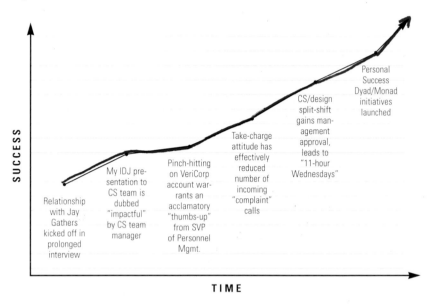

There's a story being told here. Something as undeniable and dramatic as the climbing fever-line above. There's a movement underway, a quality push as infectious as apathy and idleness once were. Senior Management has set the organization on a course to success, kicking out the stops and challenging and inspiring those who would follow. So whether tomorrow holds additional time for me in customer service, or a new role as design-group adjunct (transfer approval is still pending), my Y-axis will remain success. And, for me, success has named one of its speediest vehicles the "Inner Destination Journal."

Respectfully,

Mark Thornton

— 4 —

Attn / SysCorp Representative:

Following are a few pages I've tacked onto the end of the journal, after the summation brief. Thought you might be interested....

Regards,

Mark Thornton

Springtime again, the \span of these writings lengthens now to nearly a year, and I'm on the tenth floor laughing it all off with Rebby Conlon. Jason Pitcher's gone, I should mention--err, we aren't laughing about that, certainly, just talking it over. Either he left or was ushered out or both, depends who you ask. There were just a few closed-door discussions and then he didn't show up for Thursday's meeting and Lon was walking us through it like some social worker. Rebby hadn't known Jason all that well, I'd just mentioned it like any other news item, said it was a shame we couldn't have made room for him. What now? Who knows. Temping most likely, and he thinks there's a living he could eke out in the 'underground press,' whatever that means.

I, on the other hand, who'd been phrasing that memo to Senior Management while Pitcher braced for his exit interviews, I'm being allowed, on the strength of that memo and the "superior grasp of TQM mechanics and idiom" evidenced therein, to leave customer service for a photo-research/utility-man post in the design group. That's what Rebby and I are laughing off. The official word has just come down from Senior Management and she's called me in for the official welcome. I, who played convincingly enough at TQM to actually profit from it, am being brought into the design fold by the one person I'd let look over that brief, my co-conspirator, she saying: "Monads and Dyads, though? That was reckless," and I: "You kidding? That's what sold the thing," ho-ho, yes. Showing her that Sun Tzu bit from the journal, too:

"Just as water adapts itself to the conformation of the ground, so in war one must be flexible; he must often adapt his tactics to the enemy situation.... Under certain conditions one yields a city, sacrifices a portion of his force, or gives up ground in order to gain a more valuable objective. Such yielding therefore masks a deeper purpose, and is but another aspect of the intellectual pliancy which distinguishes the expert in war...."

Had one real nail-biter with Lon, I don't mind telling her. He'd come calling this morning: "So. Well you know they loved the

brief, the Journal program summary, you know that because you got
one of these" flapping the transfer approval in its envelope, in the
way he'd have shooed flies "And then you know, of course, they want
me to post it right up next to the charter, outside my office."

"Oh, Lon, about that," I'd said, "Traci Vendler mentioned it too,
and I told her to hold off, if they could. My point is, for a brief
that's all about teamwork, and pulling the team together, and...ehm,
leveraging team technology, but then you have one guy who's being
put up in front of the team, recognized for an individual-level contribution, do you see? There's a disconnect there, that's what I
told Traci," stammering along like that.

"Sure, well, they said it's up to you." Tap, tap, went the envelope edge on his palm, his face illegible as ever. I might have
thought he was on to me, on to the whole ruse even, if that threatened, ferret-like attentiveness weren't just the natural set of his
face....

"Relentless," Rebby's saying now, two hours later. A pine sachet
falls end-over-end in her hands. "I say let them put it up next to
the charter. Give everyone a lesson in corporate pep writing and
out-and-out farce and how you can run a company without knowing the
difference, I think that'd be a riot."

"Sure, until someone says so, and pulls the plug on the whole
thing, my transfer included--"

"Right, granted. Well if they really need to show that brief to
the public, have them wait until you're up here for good. Beyond the
reach of that whole TQM...imbroglio," selecting that word with a
raked eyebrow.

"Actually, that's something I need to ask you, when you say 'out
of reach'--"

"How safe are you going to be?"

"Right, yes."

"Well that's the question isn't it. I'll tell you this, Mark,
ever read the Decameron? All those people closed off in a country
house waiting out the plague? That's more or less what we're doing
in design, that's our approach to TQM. Scrupulous avoidance, vigilance doggedly--but quietly, humbly even--maintained. I like to
believe I was receptive to the idea at first, like anything, but the
minute they trotted out Gathers' cockamamie version of quality management I ceased being flexible about it in my mind. And I came
right out and said so, at the time. I told them I'd seen this before
and wasn't about to subject my group to it. And if you try that damn

objection cycle on me, I said, I'll have my resignation in before you're up to the couldn't-agree-with-me-more part."

"You actually—"

"Oh I came out swinging. But this was months ago, half a year ago. With discretion and valor being what they are, you know, we've grown more fond of a passive resistance approach for the day-to-day. Which means we sacrifice to them, we have to now and then, but only a little, keep the gods from rioting. They want a charter, fine, we'll send one down, may not be on the date (or in the form) they expect but so long as we make the gesture we can all have our cake. At the same time they know how I feel, though, and I remind them of that when I need to, if I threatened to pull down the whole house of cards on floor 10, just over this, I'd mean it."

"They—"

"So the answer to your question is no, they can't afford to have me storm out, not right now where they're going through a soft period and we're putting up numbers like we've been. You'll say 'yeah but if the positions were reversed...'" Rebby's thumbs spread out behind the sachet and she sucks some air in along the sides of her teeth. "Who knows. But we've got our own little self-contained economy up here and it happens to be cycling high, and the projections are strong enough, obviously, for me to be making new hires."

"Fine, I get the picture. And I'm glad to hear that, very glad. Of course you'd never guess there was any kind of stalemate situation, not from the way they act downstairs."

"No, in fact, and this you'd appreciate, Mark—they told me I could hole up for now if I liked but that eventually I'd have to give in to the demands of you youngsters."

"That sounds more like it. Your own staff was going to rise up and demand some TQM...."

"Bottom-up, inside-out quality revolution, get used to it. Totally dead-pan, they told me this. This is how all you young 'uns—and I think they actually used the term 'Generation X,' which is another reason I'm taking their word for this—this is the language you guys use—"

"—oh, yes—"

"—or you're going to use it once you learn it, this would be your toolkit for reconstructing the organization. So, if I wasn't going to give my juniors the respect that TQM reserves for them they—you—were going to swarm up and take it from me."

So we have some laffs over that too and then she's saying "anyway, enough. Well." She puts the sachet aside and has a good stare at me. "You must be feeling...yes, I can tell you are."

If she means a little giddy, I am. Flapping away like this, laughing off TQM, gearing up for a new start on my career—feeling kind of out-of-body, to be honest.

"Don't worry about it, please, you're entitled," she sez. "I'd expect anyone in your position to be somewhat...flushed."

Which is good because I can't seem to help myself. Success is said to lend the body a glow and it's true, but your first real run-in on the job, this is like insobriety. Feels like I'm about to mark off the past, which I would call a slow unfolding of pointless challenges and setbacks, just one set of ungovernable circumstances following on another, from the future, where I might actually have a hand in events. Like the day's arriving where I'll be able to divide the years of preparation and delay from a sojourn's original steps. Given, the destination's a provisional one: a career in photography? Who knows. But destinations in general seem as real to the natural world as compass points. For now there's enough assurance in the feeling, this heady kind of certainty, of having taken command of a situation I'd thought to be intractable and having advanced myself, for once, in the right direction. Which is how something as banal as an interdepartmental transfer would seem like...well, like a first emergence of destiny. Okay, have to excuse me here. Insobriety, like I say.

"No, no," sez Rebby, who seems well-used to dealing with entry-level hires and their goofy new revelations, "enjoy this, remember it. Go on out there, talk to some of those people, soak it in.... Oh and take this sachet out of here, will you? Throw it away, somewhere in the hall, god this whole office smells like some...awful, pine...thing."

Wandering through the studio, then, even introducing myself around, yes, I'll be joining up in a matter of weeks, three actually, yes, well only part-time for the first couple, then full-time, Mark Thornton—I think we met once before, at the outing? Can they tell I'm waving to them off of some parade float? Wild-eyed, walking through here as if through a fugue, into a dream office, models and movie stars bustling through

reception, doors parting automatically and a perfect cup of coffee
finding its way to my hand; no walls, just the natural channels of
foot traffic, furniture shuttled around in loose constellations as
groups convene and disband, a level of excitement near to uproar; completion, purpose, realization in whatever it is I'm doing—flipping
through stock books, lugging tripods in and out of vans, clamping neg-
atives into their carriers, anything....

Then I tell myself: it must be that the soul
has some secret, sufficient way of knowing
that it is immortal, that its vast, encompassing
circle can take in all, can accomplish all.

Beyond my anxiety, beyond this writing,
the universe waits, inexhaustible, inviting.

Jorge Borges

"Homo duplex, homo duplex!" writes Alphonse Daudet. "The first time that I perceived that I was
two was at the death of my brother, Henri, when my father cried out so dramatically, 'He is dead, he
is dead!' While my first self wept, my second self thought, 'How truly given was that cry, how fine it
would be at the theatre.' I was then fourteen years old.

"This horrible duality has often given me matter for reflection. Oh, this terrible second me, always
seated whilst the other is on foot, acting, living, suffering, bestirring itself. This second me that I
have never been able to intoxicate, to make shed tears, or put to sleep. And how it sees into things,
and how it mocks!"

REF. NO. *8 8*)   AUTHOR(S)   **Alphonse Daudet, in William James**

Back in CS not five minutes later. Handing over my accounts,
filling out some forms, the details of transition. Can concentrate
on nothing of course. No immediate call to do anything either, not
right away, which is why I don't bring up my e-mail for another
half hour. It's when I do that I notice, well I'm scanning through
a message that went to Lon, cc'ed to me, who from? Why, from Senior
Management, congratulations on the transfer, okay, they're excited
about this and that. Ah——and hold on a minute——

/44

To: Lon.Baffert (lbaffert@digigraph.com)
From: Senior.Management (admin@digigraph.com)
Subject: Continual Improvement
Cc: Rebecca.Conlon (rconlon@digigraph.com); Mark.Thornton
    (mthornton@digigraph.com)
Bcc:
X-Attachments:

Lon:

The climate here is one of excitement as we gear up to partner with SysCorp and to roll out the TQM Employee Journal program. Thanks go again to Mark Thornton for his efforts on this front, and congratulations on his transfer into the design group— Rebecca's team, we think, will profit in many ways from his initiative.

We'd like to arrange for a Journal kickoff meeting, to include representatives of the Senior staff, yourself, Rebecca and Mark. Please block out some time for late in the week of the 22nd—specific time, date and location TBD. At issue here will be the pre-liminaries of Journal implementation strategy, role-creation for the various key players, sequencing, and gauging and building on employee receptivity. We'll also begin fixing time and price points to critical process stages. And we'll be making official some excit-ing new responsibilities for Mark, our current TQM stand-out.

Re: that last point, this communiqué is an early heads-up for Mark. We've agreed on the following:

A. That Mr. Thornton

  1. be impaneled on a Journal Implementation Committee of 8 to 10 Senior and middle-management volunteers, to convene prior to business hours on the sec-ond Monday of each implementation month; and

  2. partner with appropriate team managers, as requested, to aid implementation as teams undergo the program on a staggered basis;

B. That Mr. Thornton be included in the Wednesday and Thursday evening seminars for Track 2 facilitation training. Though we would not ordinarily have considered a junior-level employee for this intensive program we feel that:

  1. his recent advancements in continual improvement more than qualify him; and that

  2. the techniques he will be exposed to, and expected to practice, will provide a much-needed advantage to the design team, a team that has struggled to keep pace with the company's "whirlwind" quality push. We expect Ms. Conlon to avail herself of Mark's advanced training in a way she has thus far hesitated to do on her own, to rededicate the design team to TQM, and to begin bringing their practices into line with those of the rest of the organization;

C. And finally, we ask that Mr. Thornton prepare a brief one-time presentation, based on his Journal summary memorandum, as part of a forthcoming meeting (date TBD) with internal management, Dr. Gathers, and representatives from SysCorp. We expect Mr. Thornton will want to detail his own history with the program, and prepare to field questions on the journal, its place in an overall TQM commitment, and the "Success Dyad and -Monad" models he's found instrumental to his personal quality quest.

Much excitement, again, on this end as we gear up for the TQM Journal program. And with the excitement, responsibility. We build the three-legged table with any commitment that's less-than-total, that is not shared company-wide, and that is not a commitment to our future.

It is precisely he who is becoming who cannot endure the state of becoming: he is too impatient for it. The youth refuses to wait until, after long study, suffering and deprivation, his picture of men and things is completed: instead he accepts on trust another that stands finished and is offered to him as though it is bound to provide him in advance with the lines and colours of *his* picture; he casts himself on to the bosom of a philosopher or poet and then has for long to deny himself and serve as a vassal. He learns much in the process: but often a youth forgets while doing so what is most worth learning and knowing: himself; he remains a partisan all his life. Alas, much boredom has to be overcome, much sweat expended, before we discover our own colours, our own brush, our own canvas!—And even then we are far from being a master of our own art of living—but at least we are master in our own workshop.

| REF. NO. 89) | *See notes, pp. 148-151* | AUTHOR(S) | **Friedrich Nietzsche** |

While taking the whole process of education into its scope, Nietzsche's observations should also dissuade you from taking anyone's counsel or adopting anyone's ideas (including ours) rashly.

146

There ain't no answer.
There ain't going to be any answer.
There never has been an answer.
That's the answer.

— Gertrude Stein

NOTES

. . . .

I. 9:34 AM

1. Friedrich Nietzsche, "On the Uses and Abuses of History," *Unmodern Observations*, translated by William Arrowsmith (New Haven, 1990).

2. Walter Wyckoff, in "What Makes a Life Significant?" in *Pragmatism and Other Essays*, by William James (New York, 1963).

3. Karen Kingston, *Creating Sacred Space with Feng Shui* (New York, 1997).

4. Nitin Nohria and James D. Berkley, "Whatever Happened to the Take-Charge Manager?" *Harvard Business Review*, January-February 1994.

5. Ralph Waldo Emerson, *Selected Writings of Ralph Waldo Emerson*, edited by William H. Gilman (New York, 1983).

6. Marsha Sinetar, *Do What You Love, the Money Will Follow: Discovering Your Right Livelihood* (New York, 1989).

7. John Micklethwait and Adrian Wooldridge, *The Witch Doctors: Making Sense of the Management Gurus* (New York, 1996).

8. Eileen C. Shapiro, *Fad Surfing in the Boardroom: Managing in the Age of Instant Answers* (Reading, Mass., 1997).

9. Micklethwait and Wooldridge, *The Witch Doctors*.

10. Samuel B. Griffith, introduction to *Sun Tzu: The Art of War* (New York, 1971).

11. Juran Institute Inc., *Juran Quality Improvement Teams* (Wilton, CT, 1993).

12. Thomas Merton, "The Empty Boat," after Chuang-tzu in *The Way of Chuang-tzu* (New York, 1969).

13. Chris Argyris, "Good Communication That Blocks Learning," *Harvard Business Review*, July-August 1994.

14. Rainmaker Inc., excerpted from "Xers Mark the Workplace," *USA Today*, by Stephanie Armour, 13 October 1997.

15. Lotte Bailyn, Joyce K. Fletcher and Deborah Kolb, "Unexpected Connections: Considering Employees' Personal Lives Can Revitalize Your Business," *Sloan Management Review*, Summer 1997.

16. Mihaly Csikszentmihalyi, *The Evolving Self: A Psychology for the Third Millennium* (New York, 1993).

17. J. Walker Smith and Ann Clurman (Yankelovich Partners, Inc.), *Rocking the Ages: The Yankelovich Report on Generational Marketing* (New York, 1997).

18. Gustave Flaubert, *Sentimental Education*, translated by Robert Baldick (New York, 1964).

19. Anthony de Mello, "The Golden Eagle," in *The Song of the Bird* (New York, 1984). .

20. Emerson, *Selected Writings of Ralph Waldo Emerson*

21. Excerpted from *The Wall Street Journal,* 22 October 1996.

22. Leah Ryan, "Temp Time Frame," *Temp Slave,* no. 10, 1997.

23. T George Harris, "The Post-Capitalist Executive: An Interview with Peter F. Drucker," *Harvard Business Review*, May-June 1993.

24. Charles Handy, *Beyond Certainty: The Changing Worlds Of Organizations* (Boston, 1996).

25. Bruce A. Pasternack, Shelley S. Keller and Albert J. Viscio, "People Power and the New Economy," *Strategy & Business*, second quarter, no. 7, 1997.

26. Shapiro, *Fad Surfing in the Boardroom*.

27. Stephen R. Covey, *The Seven Habits of Highly Effective People: Restoring the Character Ethic* (New York, 1990).

28. Steven Pinker, *How the Mind Works* (New York, 1997).

29. Argyris, *Harvard Business Review*, July-August 1994.

30. Pinker, *How the Mind Works*.

31. Jean de La Fontaine, "The Farmer and His Sons," in *La Fontaine Selected Fables*, translated by James Michie (New York, 1979).

32. Hugo Ball, "Dada Manifesto," in *Flight out of Time: A Dada Diary*, translated by Ann Raimes (Berkeley, Calif., 1996).

II. Intermezzo: Lunch at Mr. Hsu's

33. Henry David Thoreau, "Walking," in *Essays English and American*, edited by Charles W. Eliot (New York, 1938).

III. Snappin' the Crackers

34. John Micklethwait and Adrian Wooldridge, *The Witch Doctors: Making Sense of the Management Gurus* (New York, 1996).

35. Ibid.

36. Stephen R. Covey, *The Seven Habits of Highly Effective People: Restoring the Character Ethic* (New York, 1990).

37. Deepak Chopra, *The Seven Spiritual Laws of Success: A Practical Guide to the Fulfillment of Your Dreams* (San Rafael, Calif., 1994).

38. Sydney Smith, in *Money Talks: The 2500 Greatest Business Quotes from Aristotle to DeLorean*, edited by Robert W. Kent (New York, 1985). First published in *Sketches of Moral Philosophy* (1850).

39. T George Harris, "The Post-Capitalist Executive: An Interview with Peter F. Drucker," *Harvard Business Review*, May-June 1993.

40. Albert Camus, "The Myth of Sisyphus," from *The Myth of Sisyphus and other Essays*, translated by Justin O'Brien (New York, 1967).

41. William James, *The Principles of Psychology* (New York, 1950).

42. Anthony de Mello, "The Contented Fisherman," in *The Song of the Bird* (New York, 1984).

43. Marcel Proust, quoted in *How Proust Can Change Your Life: Not a Novel*, by Alain de Botton (New York, 1997).

44. Steven Pinker, *How the Mind Works* (New York, 1997).

45. Abraham Maslow, *Motivation and Personality* (New York, 1954).

46. Friedrich Nietzsche, "On the Uses and Disadvantages of History for Life," in *Untimely Meditations*, translated by R. J. Hollingdale (Cambridge, U.K., 1997).

47. Camus, *The Myth of Sisyphus*.

48. Friedrich Nietzsche, "On the Uses and Abuses of History," *Unmodern Observations*, translated by William Arrowsmith (New Haven, 1990).

49. Joe Queenan, "Failure Chic," *Forbes ASAP*, 2 June 1997.

50. Leon Botstein, *Jefferson's Children: Education and the Promise of the Future* (New York, 1997).

51. Barbara Dafoe Whitehead, "Dan Quayle Was Right," *The Atlantic*, April 1993.

52. Nietzsche, *Untimely Meditations*.

53. Proust, in *How Proust Can Change Your Life*.

54. attributed to Ralph Waldo Emerson (cited October 14, 1997), available from http://www.cascss.unt.edu/~wpalmer/emerson.htm; WORLD WIDE WEB.

55. Abraham Maslow, *Motivation and Personality* (New York, 1954).

56. Gustave Flaubert, *Sentimental Education*, translated by Robert Baldick (New York, 1964).

57. Rainer Maria Rilke, *Letters to a Young Poet*, translated by Joan M. Burnham (San Rafael, Calif., 1992).

58. Thomas Merton, *No Man Is an Island* (New York, 1983).

59. Flaubert, *Sentimental Education*.

60. Lotte Bailyn, quoted in "Integrating Work and Life: A Conversation with Lotte Bailyn," *Radcliffe Public Policy Institute Newsletter*, Fall 1997.

61. Robert Frost, "Two Tramps in Mud Time," in *Robert Frost's Poems*, introduction by Louis Untermeyer (New York, 1971).

62. Flaubert, *Sentimental Education*.

63. Ralph Waldo Emerson, "Self-Reliance," in *Essays and English Traits*, edited by Charles W. Eliot (New York, 1937).

64. Plato, *Plato's Republic*, in *Dialogues of Plato*, Jowett Translation, edited by Justin D. Kaplan (New York, 1951).

65. Walt Whitman, "When I Heard the Learn'd Astronomer," in *Selections from Leaves of Grass* (New York, 1961).

66. Ralph Waldo Emerson, "New England Reformers," in *Essays and English Traits*, edited by Charles W. Eliot (New York, 1937).

67. E. F. Schumacher, *Good Work* (New York, 1979).

68. Richard Nelson Bolles, *What Color Is Your Parachute?: A Practical Manual for Job-Hunters & Career-Changers* (New York, 1995).

69. Shunryu Suzuki, *Zen Mind, Beginner's Mind* (New York, 1994).

70. Marsha Sinetar, *Do What You Love, the Money Will Follow: Discovering Your Right Livelihood* (New York, 1987).

71. Botstein, *Jefferson's Children*.

72. J. Walker Smith and Ann Clurman (Yankelovich Partners, Inc.), *Rocking the Ages: The Yankelovich Report on Generational Marketing* (New York, 1997).

73. Judith S. Wallerstein and Sandra Blakeslee, *Second Chances: Men, Women, and Children a Decade after Divorce* (New York, 1989).

74. Smith and Clurman (Yankelovich Partners, Inc.), *Rocking the Ages*.

75. Barbara Dafoe Whitehead, *The Divorce Culture* (New York, 1997).

76. Bruce Tulgan, *Managing Generation X: How to Bring Out the Best in Young Talent* (Santa Monica, Calif., 1995).

77. Smith and Clurman (Yankelovich Partners, Inc.), *Rocking the Ages*.

78. Whitehead, *The Divorce Culture*.

79. Marcel Proust, from his novel, "In Search of Lost Time," quoted in *How Proust Can Change Your Life,* by Alain de Botton (New York, 1997).

IV. Jay Gathers' TQM Travelling TQM Dumb Show

80. James Champy, "Loony-Tunes Management Training," *Forbes*, 17 November 1997.

81. John Micklethwait and Adrian Wooldridge, *The Witch Doctors: Making Sense of the Management Gurus* (New York, 1996).

82. F. Scott Fitzgerald, "The Crack-Up," in *The Crack-Up*, edited by Edmund Wilson (New York, 1993).

83. Franz Kafka, *The Diaries: 1910-1923*, edited by Max Brod (New York, 1976).

84. Mihaly Csikszentmihalyi, *Flow: The Psychology of Optimal Experience* (New York, 1991).

85. Abraham Maslow, "Preface to the Second Edition," in *Motivation and Personality* (New York, 1987). First published in *Motivation and Personality*, (New York, 1970).

86. Steven Pinker, *How the Mind Works* (New York, 1997).

87. Marcel Proust, *By Way of Sainte-Beuve*, translated by Sylvia Townsend Warner (London, 1984).

V. Epilogue

88. Alphonse Daudet, in *The Varieties of Religious Experience: A Study in Human Nature*, by William James (New York, 1961).

89. Friedrich Nietzsche, *Human, All Too Human: A Book for Free Spirits*, translated by R. J. Hollingdale (Cambridge, U.K., 1996).

REFERENCES

. . . .

Ackroyd, Peter. 1984. *T. S. Eliot: A Life*. New York: Simon & Schuster.

Adams, Scott. 1997. *The Dilbert Future: Thriving on Stupidity in the 21st Century*. New York: HarperBusiness.

———. 1997. *The Dilbert Principle: A Cubicle's-Eye View of Bosses, Meetings, Management Fads & Other Workplace Afflictions*. New York: HarperBusiness.

Argyris, Chris. 1994. Good Communication That Blocks Learning. *Harvard Business Review* 72, no. 4.

Armour, Stephanie. 1997. Xers Mark the Workplace. *USA Today*, 13 October.

Bailyn, Lotte, Joyce K. Fletcher and Deborah Kolb. 1997. Unexpected Connections: Considering Employees' Personal Lives Can Revitalize Your Business. *Sloan Management Review* 38, no. 4.

Ball, Hugo. 1996. Dada Manifesto. In *Flight out of Time: A Dada Diary*. Translated by Ann Raimes. Berkeley, Calif.: University of California Press.

Blanchard, Ken and Sheldon Bowles. 1993. *Raving Fans*. New York: William Morrow & Company.

Boldt, Laurence G. 1992. *Zen and the Art of Making a Living: A Practical Guide to Career Design*. New York: Penguin.

Bolles, Richard Nelson. 1995. *What Color Is Your Parachute?: A Practical Manual for Job-Hunters & Career-Changers*. Berkeley, Calif.: Ten Speed Press.

Botstein, Leon. 1997. *Jefferson's Children: Education and the Promise of the Future*. New York: Doubleday.

Brazeau, Peter. 1983. *Parts of a World: Wallace Stevens Remembered*. New York: Random House.

Camus, Albert. 1967. *The Myth of Sisyphus and other Essays*. Translated by Justin O'Brien. New York: Alfred A. Knopf.

Carbonara, Peter. 1996. Hire for Attitude, Train for Skill. *Fast Company* (August-September), no. 4.

Champy, James. 1997. Loony-Tunes Management Training. *Forbes* 160.

Chodron, Pema. 1991. *The Wisdom of No Escape: And the Path of Loving-Kindness*. Boston: Shambhala.

Chopra, Deepak. 1994. *The Seven Spiritual Laws of Success: A Practical Guide to the Fulfillment of Your Dreams*. San Rafael, Calif.: Amber-Allen Publishing and New World Library.

Cleary, Thomas, trans. 1995. *Minding Mind: A Course in Basic Meditation*. Boston: Shambhala.

Covey, Stephen R. 1990. *The Seven Habits of Highly Effective People: Restoring the Character Ethic*. New York: Simon & Schuster.

Csikszentmihalyi, Mihaly. 1993. *The Evolving Self: A Psychology for the Third Millennium*. New York: HarperCollins.

———. 1991. *Flow: The Psychology of Optimal Experience*. New York: HarperPerennial.

De Botton, Alain. 1997. *How Proust Can Change Your Life: Not a Novel*. New York: Pantheon Books.

De Mello, Anthony. 1984. *The Song of the Bird*. New York: Image Books.

Drucker, Peter F. et al. 1997. Looking Ahead: Implications of the Present. *Harvard Business Review* 75, no. 5.

Economist, The. 1997. Service with a Smile, 344, no. 8025.

Emerson, Ralph Waldo. 1937. *Essays and English Traits*. Edited by Charles W. Eliot. New York: P. F. Collier & Son Corporation.

———. 1983. *Selected Writings of Ralph Waldo Emerson*. Edited by William H. Gilman. New York: Penguin.

Fitzgerald, F. Scott. 1993. *The Crack-Up*. Edited by Edmund Wilson. New York: New Directions.

Flaubert, Gustave. 1964. *Sentimental Education*. Translated by Robert Baldick. New York: Penguin.

Flynn, Gillian. 1996. Xers vs. Boomers: Teamwork or Trouble? *Personnel Journal* 75, no. 11.

Fulghum, Robert, comp. 1997. *Words I Wish I Wrote*. New York: HarperCollins.

Frost, Robert. 1971. *Robert Frost's Poems*. Introduction by Louis Untermeyer. New York: Washington Square Press.

Gibran, Kahlil. 1996. *The Prophet*. New York: Alfred A. Knopf.

Gowers, Andrew. 1997. Prize-Winners in the Business of Jargon. *Financial Times*, 24 November.

Griffith, Samuel B., trans. and intro. 1971. *Sun Tzu: The Art of War*. New York: Oxford University Press.

Hamel, Gary and C. K. Prahalad. 1994. *Competing for the Future*. Boston: Harvard Business School Press.

Handy, Charles. 1996. *Beyond Certainty: The Changing Worlds of Organizations*. Boston: Harvard Business School Press.

Hanh, Thich Nhat. 1987. *The Miracle of Mindfulness: A Manual on Meditation*. Boston: Beacon Press.

———. 1992. *Peace Is Every Step: The Path of Mindfulness in Everyday Life*. New York: Bantam.

Harris, T George. 1993. The Post-Capitalist Executive: An Interview with Peter F. Drucker. *Harvard Business Review* 71, no. 3.

Heskett, James, W. Earl Sasser, Jr. and Leonard A. Schlesinger. 1997. *The Service Profit Chain*. New York: The Free Press.

Highfield, Roger and Paul Carter. 1993. *The Private Lives of Albert Einstein*. New York: St. Martin's Press.

Howe, Neil and Bill Strauss. 1993. *13th Gen: Abort, Retry, Ignore, Fail?* New York: Random House.

James, William. 1995. *Pragmatism*. New York: Dover Publications.

———. 1963. *Pragmatism and Other Essays*. New York: Washington Square Press.

———. 1950. *The Principles of Psychology*. New York: Dover Publications.

———. 1961. *The Varieties of Religious Experience: A Study in Human Nature*. New York: Macmillan.

Kafka, Franz. 1976. *The Diaries: 1910-1923*. Edited by Max Brod. New York: Schocken Books.

Kao, John. 1996. *Jamming: The Art and Discipline of Business Creativity*. New York: HarperBusiness.

Kent, Robert W., ed. 1985. *Money Talks: The 2500 Greatest Business Quotes from Aristotle to DeLorean*. New York: Facts on File.

Kingston, Karen. 1997. *Creating Sacred Space with Feng Shui*. New York: Broadway Books.

La Fontaine, Jean de. 1979. *La Fontaine Selected Fables*. Translated by James Michie. New York: Viking Press.

Landman, Janet. 1993. *Regret: The Persistence of the Possible*. New York: Oxford University Press.

Lears, Jackson. 1997. Man the Machine. *The New Republic*, 1 September.

Mascaro, Juan, trans. 1986. *The Bhagavad Gita*. New York: Penguin.

———. 1965. *The Upanishads*. New York: Penguin.

Maslow, Abraham H. 1954. *Motivation and Personality*. New York: Harper.

———. 1987. Third Edition. *Motivation and Personality*. New York: HarperCollins.

———. 1968. *Toward a Psychology of Being*. New York: Van Nostrand Reinhold.

Merton, Thomas. 1983. *No Man Is an Island*. New York: Octagon Press.

———. 1969. *The Way of Chuang-tzu*. New York: New Directions Publishing.

Micklethwait, John and Adrian Wooldridge. 1996. *The Witch Doctors: Making Sense of the Management Gurus*. New York: Random House.

Nietzsche, Friedrich. 1996. *Human, All Too Human: A Book for Free Spirits*. Translated by R. J. Hollingdale. Cambridge, U.K.: Cambridge University Press.

———. 1990. *Unmodern Observations*. Translated by William Arrowsmith. New Haven: Yale University Press.

———. 1997. *Untimely Meditations*. Translated by R. J. Hollingdale. Cambridge, U.K.: Cambridge University Press.

Nohria, Nitin and James D. Berkley. 1994. Whatever Happened to the Take-Charge Manager? *Harvard Business Review* 72, no. 1.

Pasternack, Bruce A., Shelley S. Keller and Albert J. Viscio. 1997. People Power and the New Economy. *Strategy & Business* (second quarter), no. 7.

Pawel, Ernst. 1984. *The Nightmare of Reason: A Life of Franz Kafka*. New York: Farrar-Straus-Giroux.

Phillips, Michael. 1993. *The Seven Laws of Money*. Boston: Shambhala.

Pinker, Steven. 1997. *How the Mind Works*. New York: W. W. Norton & Company.

Plato. 1951. *Plato's Republic* in *Dialogues of Plato*. Jowett Translation. Edited by Justin D. Kaplan. New York: Washington Square Press.

Proust, Marcel. 1984. *By Way of Sainte-Beuve*. Translated by Sylvia Townsend Warner. London: Hogarth Press.

Queenan, Joe. 1997. Failure Chic. *Forbes ASAP*, 2 June.

Radcliffe Public Policy Institute Newsletter. 1997. Integrating Work and Life: A Conversation with Lotte Bailyn, (fall).

Reps, Paul, comp. 1989. *Zen Flesh, Zen Bones: A Collection of Zen & Pre-Zen Writings*. Rutland, Vt.: Charles Tuttle Company.

Rilke, Rainer Maria. 1992. *Letters to a Young Poet.* Translated by Joan M. Burnham. San Rafael, Calif.: New World Library.

Rowe, Chip, ed. 1997. *The Book of Zines: Readings from the Fringe.* New York: Henry Holt & Company.

Ryan, Leah. 1997. Temp Time Frame. *Temp Slave*, no. 10.

Sacks, Peter. 1996. *Generation X Goes to College.* Peru, Ill.: Open Court Trade and Academic Books.

Schumacher, E. F. 1979. *Good Work.* New York: HarperCollins.

Shah, Idries. 1989. *The Exploits of the Incomparable Mulla Nasrudin.* London: Octagon Press.

———. 1989. *The Subtleties of the Inimitable Mulla Nasrudin.* London: Octagon Press.

Shapiro, Eileen C. 1997. *Fad Surfing in the Boardroom: Managing in the Age of Instant Answers.* Reading, Mass.: Addison-Wesley.

Sher, Barbara. 1994. *I Could Do Anything If I Only Knew What It Was.* New York: Dell Publishing.

Sinetar, Marsha. 1987. *Do What You Love, the Money Will Follow: Discovering Your Right Livelihood.* New York: Dell Publishing.

Smith, J. Walker and Ann Clurman, Yankelovich Partners, Inc. 1997. *Rocking the Ages: The Yankelovich Report on Generational Marketing.* New York: HarperBusiness.

Suzuki, Shunryu. 1994. *Zen Mind, Beginner's Mind.* New York: Weatherhill.

Theophane the Monk. 1981. *Tales from a Magic Monastery.* New York: Crossroads Publishing.

Thoreau, Henry David. 1996. *Citizen Thoreau.* Ann Arbor: State Street Press.

———. 1938. Walking. *Essays English and American.* Edited by Charles W. Eliot. New York: P. F. Collier & Son Corporation.

Tulgan, Bruce. 1995. *Managing Generation X: How to Bring Out the Best in Young Talent.* Santa Monica, Calif.: Merritt Publishing.

Van Housen, Alice. 1997. Here's a Radical Idea—Tell the Truth. *Fast Company* (August-September), no. 10.

Wallerstein, Judith S. and Sandra Blakeslee. 1989. *Second Chances: Men, Women, and Children a Decade after Divorce.* New York: Ticknor & Fields.

Weber, Alan M. 1998. Is Your Job Your Calling (extended interview). *Fast Company.* (Boston, Mass.[cited January 19, 1998]). Available from http://www.fastcompany.com/youdecide; WORLD WIDE WEB. First appeared in *Fast Company,* no. 13 (February-March).

Whitehead, Barbara Dafoe. 1993. Dan Quayle Was Right. *The Atlantic* 271, no. 4.

———. 1997. *The Divorce Culture.* New York: Alfred A. Knopf.

Whitman, Walt. 1961. When I Heard the Learn'd Astronomer. *Selections from Leaves of Grass.* New York: Avenel Books.

Whitmyer, Claude, ed. 1994. *Mindfulness and Meaningful Work: Explorations in Right Livelihood.* Berkeley, Calif.: Parallax Press.

Wieseltier, Leon. 1993. Total Quality Meaning: Notes Toward A Definition of Clintonism. *The New Republic* 209, no. 3-4.

PUBLISHER'S NOTE TO THE SECOND EDITION

. . . .

Integrating work and life in the restlessness of the post-capitalist world raises important questions which, it seemed to us at Allen & Osborne anyway, had yet to be articulated by the twentysomething professionals moving from college to the workplace. While the historical angst of the young man is nothing new, today's entry-level workers are confronting an increasingly complex and fast-paced culture, with insecurities spreading rapidly among managers, and an alarming number of business gurus stepping in to offer some real, and some very unreal, solutions.

The idea for a workplace reader came from Carol Allen. That idea was seized upon by Jon Baird, who took the book from his journal concept to execution. His writing, designing and producing *Day Job* from cover to cover in a matter of nine months was an incredible achievement. Carol willingly became the collective voice of SysCorp's Greek chorus, whose asides are cut and pasted into Jon's original presentation in this multimedia scrapbook.

Mark Jacobstein, a college friend of Jon's, and Bernardo Chevez, both of iXL New York, have helped us build the *Day Job* community at www.dayjob.com. Visitors can now interact with the author and with each other here and submit writings for the follow-up edition of *Day Job*, which will be written entirely by visitors to the site. So stop by, we'd love to hear from you.

Stuart Crainer kindly introduced *Day Job* to Richard Burton and Mark Allin of Capstone Publishing. With a little help from our old friend John Kelly, they are publishing the international edition of *Day Job* as a Capstone book in January 1999. We are proud to be associated with this forward-looking British publishing house.

We have been encouraged and assisted by many people. Christian Zabriskie enthusiastically supported Jon Baird in the early stages of the book with ideas for the structure of the narrative. Jennifer Hamilton spent countless hours of research in the library and on the Internet. B.J. Beckett painstakingly scripted the annotator's notes. Natalie Reid's proofreading and thoughtful suggestions helped us to stand back from the project at a critical time in the book's development. Susan Kurtzman read the early drafts and gave us many promotional ideas. Sarah Imrie provided insights from her generation, helped with the final proofreading and later joined the firm as Marketing Director. Alex Parr, Alex McCallum, and Robert Moulthrop all read the manuscript at various stages and suggested improvements.

We would like to thank each of the sources we have drawn upon in the selections surrounding the narrative, and we hope that readers will use these references as recommendations for further reading. We are particularly indebted to John Micklethwait and Adrian Wooldridge, who graciously gave us permission to quote extensively from their book *The Witch Doctors*, by far the best book on what they call the 'teenage' discipline of management science.

Final words of thanks go to David Wilk and Susan Shaw of the LPC Group for seeing the potential of *Day Job* and arranging for its distribution in the US and Canada.

August 1998   — Laurance Allen

READER'S NOTES

READER'S NOTES

Get yourself a *Day Job*, maybe even a few.

It's easy, not to mention fun.

FOUR DIFFERENT WAYS TO GO, HERE:

❶ **TELEPHONE ORDERS**

Call 1-800-344-4501, Monday through Friday, 8am-5pm, with your credit card at the ready [Visa or MasterCard only, please].

❷ **ORDERING OVER THE INTERNET**

Visit www.dayjob.com, click the order button on the menu bar, and you're off.

❸ **FAX ORDERS**

Fill out the form on the back of this card and fax to (508) 583-9904.

❹ **MAIL ORDERS**

Fill out the form on the back of this card, cut it out where indicated, and drop in the mail. If you're sending a check or money order, please send your filled-out card (folded, if need be) and payment in an envelope to:

Allen & Osborne, Inc.
P.O. Box 339
West Bridgewater, MA 02379

- - - - - - CUT OUT ALONG DOTTED LINE - CUT OUT ALONG DOTTED LINE - - - - - -

NO POSTAGE
NECESSARY
IF MAILED
IN THE
UNITED STATES

BUSINESS REPLY MAIL
FIRST-CLASS MAIL PERMIT NO. 4 WEST BRIDGEWATER MA

POSTAGE WILL BE PAID BY ADDRESSEE

Allen & Osborne, Inc.
PO BOX 339
WEST BRIDGEWATER MA 02379-9970

Day Job
Order Form
. . . .

Total books ordered _____ **x 24.95**   = _____

Handling charge [$4.00 per book / $10.00 international]   + _____

Sales tax: Massachusetts residents
           add 5% to subtotal   + _____

TOTAL COST   = _____

Name _____   Phone _(____)_____

Organization [if applicable] _____

Street _____   City _____

State / Province _____ ZIP / Postal Code _____ Country _____

❏ Check/Money Order enclosed, payable to Allen & Osborne, Inc.

❏ Visa   ❏ MasterCard

Card Number _____   Expiration date _____

Signature _____